A

DEADLY

Voyage

Richard Allen

RICHARD ALLEN

Richard Allen is a retired senior police officer who, in
addition to uniformed duties, saw service with the CID,
the
Vice Squad, the Drug Squad and Special Branch.
Richard is the author of two best selling publications
dealing with police management and leadership,
which were listed as recommended reading by both the
US Department of Justice and the Police Staff College.

'A DEADLY Voyage' is the seventh in a
series of Superintendent Mark Faraday adventures.

By the same author

Non-fiction:

'Effective Supervision in the Police Service'

'Leading from the Middle'

Fiction:

'DIRTY Business'

'DIE Back'

'DARKER than Death'

'In the DARKEST of Shadows'

'DEADLY Inheritance'

'In the DEAD of Night'

Dedication

To a fine friend of 23 years
Geoff Rees
1924 – 2022
Flight Lieutenant RAF
Captain Qantas

to all the staff at Myeloma UK
the organisation that supports those with
Myeloma, the terminal blood/bone marrow cancer

And

to my Dearest Wife
Ann
Ever Loving, Loyal and Caring

'without your sweet love what would life be?'

'The face cannot lie.'
from *'Manwatching'* by Desmond Morris.

'The difficulty with lying
is that the sub-conscious mind acts automatically
and independently of our verbal lie, and so
our body language gives us away. The moment we begin
to lie,
the body sends out contradictory signals.'
from *'Body Language'* by Allan Pease.

Psychogenic Needs: the need for achievement,
recognition,
Respect and the avoidance of shame and ridicule.
from *'Psychology'* by Hilgard, Hilgard and Atkinson.

'It is possible that not a single one of life's experiences
is totally forgotten.'
from *'Our Own Worst Enemy'* by Professor Norman F Dixon.

Obsession: 'a persistent disturbing preoccupation with
an often unreasonable feeling.'
Merriam-Webster Dictionary (the oldest US dictionary publishers).

Envy: 'the feeling of wanting to be in the
same situation as someone else.'
Oxford English Dictionary

Chapter One

Monday, 21st October 1805.
Off Cape Trafalgar, Spain.

AT ELEVEN O'CLOCK, Vice Admiral Lord Nelson knelt in the Great Cabin of his flag ship, the one-hundred-and two-gun HMS *Victory*, below his favourite portrait of his mistress, his love, his 'Guardian Angel', his Emma, his Lady Emma Hamilton, kneeling as he wrote his prayer, a remarkable prayer full of humility and humanity:

> *'May the Great God, whom I worship, grant to my Country*
> *and for the benefit of Europe in general, a great and glorious*
> *victory; and may no misconduct in anyone tarnish it, and may*
> *humanity after victory be the predominant feature of the*
> *British Fleet. For myself, I commit my life to Him who made me,*
> *and may His blessing light upon my endeavours ...*
> *to Him I resign myself ....'*

Earlier at daybreak, with the British Fleet some nine miles to windward of the enemy so as to prevent them from fleeing to Cadiz, Nelson was on the quarter deck wearing his old undress uniform. It would take about six hours for the British Fleet to drift in the light breeze, at very much less than three knots, towards the Combined Fleet of the French and Spanish, even with all sails set in an effort to catch the weak and feeble wind.

At ten past six, the *Victory* hoisted Signal Flag Number 72: 'FORM TWO COLUMNS'. Later it would be Signal Flag Number 13: 'PREPARE FOR BATTLE' at which the drummers would 'Beat to Quarters'. With that direction the lieutenants would order 'Clear for Action' and the gun captains would order 'load', 'run out', 'prime'. Then they would simply wait. Wait in tense, nervous anticipation.

At nine o'clock, Nelson changed into his dress uniform, not his most elaborate uniform, but a more formal one none the less, its gold lace dulled by salt stains. Nor did he wear his most elaborate felt hat adorned with the stunning *chelengk* gifted to him by Sultan Selim the Third of Turkey after his tremendous victory at the Battle of the Nile in 1798, but a simple black silk rosette. Nevertheless, upon his coat Nelson wore the embroidered copies of his four Orders of Chivalry.

Nelson had been urged to cover these decorations in the knowledge that the French were employing Alpine sharpshooters, considered to be the finest marksmen in Europe, in the 'tops' with the task of bringing down English officers. But Nelson understood what was a critical element of leadership and replied that that would be impossible because he had to demonstrate 'the force of example'. He knew that as the terrifying moment of battle approached, the *Victory*, with a crew of more than eight hundred souls, half of whom were not English at all and most were illiterate, the youngest of which was 10 year old Boy First Class Johnny Doag, Nelson had to demonstrate his utter faith in the crew, a complete confidence in the abilities of his officers and an absolute certainty in the outcome of the forthcoming battle, predicting that 'I shall give them such a dressing as they never had before.'

But Nelson's plan was controversial. The accepted practice of the day was for enemy ships to adopt a 'line ahead formation' in parallel and then fire upon each other. Nelson's plan was very different. His two squadrons would sail towards the enemy at right-angles, breaking through and then turning to the left and attacking the enemy from the port side. This was a hazardous manoeuvre in the initial phase with the massed guns of the enemy facing Nelson whose ships could only reply with their two forward facing 68 pounder carronades and a few 12 pounder 'bow chasers', but, as the British ships eventually broke through between various enemy ships they were able to fire broadsides through the vulnerable stern cabins reeking bloody havoc the full length of the enemy decks and then to swing to fire withering broadsides upon broadsides into the enemy's unprepared starboard side at a fire rate of one every 90 seconds, three times that of the Combined Fleet due to meticulous training.

At 12.15, the enemy fired its first ranging shot at HMS *Victory,* their sixth shot puncturing her main top gallant sail. The enemy now had her range and the *Victory's* sails became pock-marked with holes with five of the enemy pouring concentrated fire upon her. One shot cut Nelson's secretary, Scott, in half as he talked to Captain

Hardy at Nelson's side and a few moments later a jagged spear-like splinter of wood struck Hardy's left silver shoe buckle. The captain's clerk, Whipple, was cut down shortly after, just one of the fifty-seven who would be killed that day aboard the *Victory* along with one hundred and two wounded. For some twenty minutes the British ships could not return any meaningful fire from their 12, 24 and 32-pounders yet they kept, without hesitation, their determined course towards the enemy.

The Combined Fleet of French and Spanish ships was formidable with thirty-four sail of the line compared to Nelson's twenty-seven, added to which their fleet included the two largest and most powerful warships in the world, the *Santissima Trinidad* and the *Santa Anna.*

As the British Fleet approached the enemy, the *Victory* raised Signal Flags Number 1 and Number 6: 'ENGAGE THE ENEMY MORE CLOSELY', signals that remained flying from the masthead until the mast itself fell, flying not as a reprimand but reminding every captain to 'put your ship alongside the enemy, you can do no wrong'. The *Victory* broke through the enemy line between the *Bucentaure* and the *Redoutable*, their rigging to become locked in a death grip as their hulls ground together. The fighting raged around Nelson and Hardy as the *Victory's* wheel was shattered and her mizzen mast shot away as she also engaged the mighty *Santissima Trinidad.* The battle was intense, not only as the *Victory* continued to engage the enemy ships at close quarters, but throughout the fleet, yet Nelson was calm and composed commenting: 'This is too warm work, Hardy, to last long.'

At 1.15, Hardy turned towards Nelson and realised he was alone only to see that the admiral was on his knees propping himself up with his left hand for a fleeting moment only to collapse upon the blood-stained sand of the deck.

Captain Hardy quickly ran to Nelson. 'Hardy, I believe they have done for me at last,' he said.

Although in great pain, Nelson continued to give orders as they clumsily carried their admiral down the steep steps through the Middle Deck, the Lower Deck then to the Orlop situated below the waterline where the surgeon, Mr Beatty, and his assistants operated in what was described as a 'butcher's shambles'. The Orlop was dark, airless and evil smelling, filled with the pleas of desperate anticipation and the cries of terrifying physical horror mingled with ominous silence as William Beatty performed his grizzly duty. They propped Nelson up on the port side just forward of the after-hanging magazine and rigged a 'fighting lantern' from a beam above him. They removed his shirt and, in so doing, exposed his gold necklace and a miniature portrait of Emma, Lady Hamilton.

The musket ball, weighing less than twenty-two grams, had entered Nelson's chest through his left epaulette, broken two ribs, severed the pulmonary artery, fractured the sixth and seventh dorsal vertebrae and severed his spinal cord, yet, although in intense pain he continued to ask questions and required to be regularly updated on the progress of the battle, a battle he was constantly reminded of as the 32-pounder cannons on the deck immediately above him rumbled and careered back and forth and the great ship shuddered as they fired and received shot that could penetrate three feet of English oak.

'How goes the battle? How many ships have we taken?' Nelson asked.

'Fourteen or fifteen, my Lord,' replied Hardy.

'I had hoped for more. At least twenty.' He questioned further: 'I hope none of our ships have struck?' he asked, seeking confirmation that no British ship had surrendered.

'No, my Lord, there is no fear of that.'

The ferocious battle continued to rage during which a French attack swarming across *Victory's* decks was beaten back. The dead and the wounded lay everywhere amongst the debris of war, the miles of tangled rigging and acres of tattered sail that the *Victory* bore; the broken spars, upended cannon, and the discarded cutlasses, sea axes and flintlocks of the dead, as the *Victory* racked the *Bucentaure* with her broadsides. The battle raged on as more enemy ships struck their colours. Eventually, the progress of the battle became clear, the outcome certain.

It would be victory. A stunning victory, with only four of the enemy eventually left seaworthy and no British ships destroyed or taken.

And so it was that at 4.30pm, at the moment of a resounding victory that would secure Britain's supremacy at sea for a hundred years, the ship's log recorded that Admiral Lord Nelson, in great pain, uttered his last words:

'Thank God I have done my duty.'

Chapter Two

Friday, 5th and Saturday, 6th April 2019.
Victoria and Vancouver, British Columbia, Canada.

THE GRAND PIANO was being played with soothing clarity. In no way did it dominate the entrance foyer but seemed to envelope those who entered with a calmness. They did not know the name of the tune, but that didn't matter at all – it was 'easy listening' – the perfect beginning for the long-awaited dream holiday for Chief Superintendent Mark Faraday and his wife, Detective Superintendent Kay Yin. Their suite on the 8th floor of the Shangri-La hotel on West Georgia Street was ideal with views towards the Inlet. Cut flowers - eucalyptus, gladioli and stocks, had been placed in a neat glass vase along with a tray of chocolates on the central table with a personalised note of welcome from the general manager.

Mark and Kay had an early snack lunch in the *Chiyoda* on Alberni Street overlooking Brockton Point. They had plenty of time for relaxation and had already arranged to meet with a Canadian police colleague through the IPA, the International Police Association, the organisation established in 1959 in the UK which provided, amongst other things, world-wide links to officers and their families, particularly for those on holiday. As a result they met with Superintendent Richard Marsh of the Royal Canadian Mounted Police at Coal Harbour who greeted them resplendent in the force's traditional uniform of scarlet tunic, blue breeches with yellow trouser pipping and oxblood riding boots which had their origins way, way back in 1873.

They shook hands, standing on the board walk, the salt air breeze in their hair and the sun on their faces. But, as they gossiped, Kay and Mark were distracted and smiled with anticipation and delight as they walked along the board walk towards a shimmering silver-grey float plane tethered to the quay. Superintendent Marsh introduced them to the aircraft's owner 'Flight' Hargreaves.

'There are over fifty aerial tour companies operating out of Vancouver,' explained 'Flight', 'most of which use the latest luxury single or twin De Havilland turbo prop *Otters*, but I'm reliably informed that you are often unconventional and would probably like an aircraft that was a little more adventurous?'

'We can do adventurous,' replied Mark as he and Kay looked expectantly at the tethered float plane.

'Well that's good because Richard here thought you might prefer a trip in this 1947 De Havilland *Beaver* of mine'. 'Flight' gestured towards the sturdy silver-grey aircraft with its powerful single radial engine clearly visible under its cowling. Old as it may have been, it exuded power and robustness.

'Wow,' said Kay with excitement, 'it looks like something from an Indiana Jones film.'

'This is brilliant,' said Mark, 'absolutely brilliant.'

'Okay, then let's get on board and get you guys strapped in,' said 'Flight' - but not before a smiling group photograph – actually six photographs.

They clambered up onto the floats and ducked inside. The doors were closed, and they settled into comfortable seats and donned headphones, then the nine-cylinder four stroke radial engine cranked into life as each cylinder engaged and belched just a little smoke, the 450hp engine quickly adopting a steady solid throbbing rhythm as she moved away from the quay. They awaited clearance mid-channel, then the engine roared as 'Flight' applied full throttle and they surged forward bumping and bouncing through the exhilarating spray of take-off.

The smooth flight lasted a little over forty minutes, with 'Flight' giving a commentary as the high wings allowing for the uninterrupted panoramic views of Vancouver, the beaches and parks and the North Shore Mountains with 'Flight' taking every opportunity to skilfully bank his aircraft so as to provide Mark and Kay with the very best views of his home of which he was clearly so proud. The views were breath-taking, and the flight was one of those 'never to be forgotten' experiences.

For 'Flight' the ownership of the *Beaver* and flying were the pinnacle of his ambitions. He had a good life. He had no envy for those pilots flying a *Typhoon* jet fighter or an *A380* carrying over five hundred passengers. On a daily basis he was fulfilling his boyhood dream. He would never be wealthy, but he was content. He was blessed, sharing with others the magic of the air, the scenery and his world.

Much later they travelled to the Empress Hotel on Victoria Island for Afternoon Tea in the Lobby Lounge. 'Taking tea' in the Lobby Lounge was a 'must do' experience rather like taking tea at Raffles Hotel in Singapore, Reids in Madeira or The Savoy in London.

The Lobby Lounge was cool and airy, with tall walls and white ceilings. The atmosphere was serene, disturbed only by harmonious babble, as they were guided to their table between white Greek Corinthian pillars and miniature pines. They attracted attention. Mark 6' 4" tall, 38 years of age, dark wavy hair and sharp brown eyes and Kay, 5' 3" tall, 33 years of age, petite with a graceful Oriental beauty that captivated. Once seated, they began to relax, something impossible to do back home in England during a short weekend break. England seemed a world away which, of course, it was. They spoke of their plans for the evening and the following day but, needless to say, the conversation between these two police officers inevitably drifted towards the notoriety surrounding the hotel's architect, Francis Rattenbury.

Rattenbury was born in 1867 in the UK but emigrated to Canada in 1891. He quickly gained a reputation as a fine and sought-after architect who designed many prestigious buildings including the Empress Hotel and the Parliament Building in Victoria. He became rich. However, in 1922 he met the vivacious twenty-seven year old Alma Pakenham, a concert pianist who, during the Great War had driven ambulances behind enemy lines and was awarded the French Croix de Guerre for her bravery. Alma could be described as a *femme fatale*, a woman that most men would find difficult to resist. Rattenbury, now 56, did not find her difficult to resist at all. Far from it. In fact, he divorced his wife, Florence, and married the alluring Alma. Today, this sort of behaviour would scarcely be noted but in 1925 it was considered scandalous. As a result, Rattenbury was shunned, and his architectural contracts ended. Consequently, in 1927 he and Alma travelled to live in England and he set up home in the sea-side town of Bournemouth with Alma, the Rolls-Royce and George Stoner, their 18 year old chauffeur.

During the evening of 22nd March 1935 Francis Rattenbury was seated in front of the fire in their lounge with his bed-time cup of cocoa. This nightly ritual was brutally interrupted by George striking Francis over the head numerous times with a heavy wooden mallet. In those days, small provincial police forces would call in 'The Yard' to investigate murders.

It had been a crime of the obsessed that defied logic and reason, one that would have been difficult to excuse or conceal from the Scotland Yard detectives and it didn't take them long to place George and Alma under arrest. They were both charged with murder and appeared at the Old Bailey. Alma was defended by the eminent KC, Ewen Montagu, who later gained fame as the war-time mastermind of the remarkably successful deception plan 'Operation Mincemeat'. He was equally successful in his defence of Alma, although it probably helped that the all-male jury also found Alma difficult to resist. George was not so fortunate. He was found guilty and sentenced to death. Ironically, a day before his execution George's sentence was commuted to Life Imprisonment although a distressed Alma climbed onto the bridge over the River Stour in Christchurch, stabbed herself in the chest a number of times, fell into the river and drowned. George served only seven years. On his release he returned to live in Bournemouth until his death at the age of 83 in 2000.

Crimes of interest seemed to follow Mark and Kay. Or, more accurately, they seemed to follow them. Whatever, in the daily newspapers they read, whilst eating the cucumber and salmon sandwiches, scones, savoury treats and patisseries, of the spectacular interceptions of drug smugglers in the English Channel by British Border Force cutters and the National Crime Agency. The drugs recovered had a street value of £73 million.

'Wow, a good operation by Border Force and the NCA,' remarked Kay lightly. 'That will put the cat amongst the pigeons.'

Attentive waiting staff seemed to appear as if on cue. 'Madam,' suggested the waiter, 'if you wish I will clear some of your plates, much better for your papers.'

'Thank you,' replied Kay with a captivating smile.

As the waiter moved away, Mark continued their conversation. 'It certainly will.' Mark glanced towards Kay, 'and the drug barons won't tolerate that sort of failure.'

'No, they certainly won't,' agreed Kay knowingly, thinking back to her time as a Drug Squad detective. 'They will make an example of someone for the failure and unpleasant retribution will surely follow as a punishment, as an example to others. I wouldn't want to be in their shoes.'

'I definitely wouldn't,' said Mark as he remembered some of the hideous repercussions meted out to those who had failed. 'Now they will have to make up that loss to their customers pretty quickly to ensure that they maintain their reputation and contracts.'

'Yes,' agreed Kay, 'others will be gloating and eagerly gathering in the wings to expand their business and fill any vacuum in the interruption of supplies that this will create, you can be absolutely sure of that.'

'But at least nothing for *us* to worry about for the next few weeks,' said Mark with a beaming smile. 'It is a world away, isn't it?'

'Yes,' she said enthusiastically, '*we* are on holiday.' She leant over and hugged her husband. But, had Kay spoken too soon?

'Would you care for more tea, madam?' enquired a waitress.

***

Today, the 6th, they visited the Gastown District and Chinatown. They attracted no attention in Chinatown, the third largest Chinatown in north America, which simply teemed with jostling Chinese and Europeans amongst the multitude of colourful paper lanterns, the festoons of bright lights and inviting stalls. There was an excited bustle everywhere as they moved through the food markets decked with fresh fruit and vegetables, meats and fish, and surrounded by the tantalising combination of aromas of the Oriental dishes. The inquisitive and eager customers at the antique, art and gift stalls, jewellery and silk shops were everywhere, babbling, often excitedly, mainly in English and Cantonese or a mixture of both. Mark and Kay were full of smiles. Everywhere there was something curious to see and Kay was able to explain some of the customs, and their religious and traditional significances, and this certainly applied to the food. It was impossible to ignore the aroma of the food stalls and they could not resist sampling dim sum, aromatic duck, satay chicken on bamboo skewers, spring rolls, prawns in Szechuan sauce and prawn crackers.

'Reminds you of home?' said Mark.

'Yes ... happier days,' she reflected with a certain sadness on how Hong Kong had changed. She put her arm in his and hugged, reassured to be with him as they made their way back to their hotel.

***

It was two o'clock when the taxi dropped them at Canada Place on the Burrand Inlet. On time for embarkation. Two hours prior to departure. Check-in was smooth and efficient. Their boarding and stateroom key passes were in the form of a wristwatch, or a brooch if preferred, named *MyWay* that allowed access to the ship, payments at the on-board boutiques in *The Strand* and on *Bond Street,* or booking a restaurant or shore excursion whilst on board their ship, the *Tranquillity*. It was all very efficient and trouble-free. They made their way up the gently sloping glass-covered gangway to be greeted by a ship's officer in pristine white shirt-sleeve order uniform who directed them towards the champagne in the main atrium under a magnificent Venetian *Miame* glass ceiling centrepiece. Although bustling, the atmosphere created in the atrium was welcoming, calm and relaxed against a background of soft classical music. It was almost magical.

The *Tranquillity* was a British registered ship, operating out of Southampton and intended primarily for British passengers. She was certainly not a mega-liner, she was described as 'boutique, beautiful and classical'. A little over forty-three thousand tonnes, with seven hundred and three cabins, which were usually referred to as 'staterooms', a description that seemed to make some people feel much more important. There were only one thousand and seventeen passengers and a crew of five hundred and forty-two. The *Tranquillity* had eleven lounges and bars, a theatre, a cinema, two swimming pools, a spa and beauty salon, hairdressers, a multi-gym, a library and five restaurants, but no climbing walls or water shoots, just the opportunity for peacefully pampered relaxation which was what Mark and Kay wanted on this twenty-nine-day cruise.

But there was little relaxation on the quayside. It was if someone had poked a stick into a Dolichoderus Mariae ant hill. Just energetic but orderly activity with purpose. They both peered over the varnished teak rails on the Promenade Deck. Below, a multitude of grey, red and green steel containers lined the quay parallel to the ship's side, containers filled with everything from toilet rolls to sacks of potatoes, cans of beer to net bags of carrots, onions and apples, pallets of milk and eggs. Porters and chefs stood ready. They saw one rather portly chef, a tall *toque blanche* adorning his head, take a knife from his pocket and gesture to a junior who removed the top crate of pineapples from a stack of six. The chef surveyed the contents before removing one. He held it in his hand, smelt it passionately to savour its freshness then cut around the top to remove a slice of the fruit which he carefully tasted. Moments passed. Juniors paid awe-inspired attention to the portly chef and awaited instructions. Satisfied as to its quality, the chef moved to a second tier of crates containing bright oranges, then a third of apricots. On each occasion he repeated his process of inspection. He was a busy man but fastidious and attentive.

A ship's officer, two and a half gold bars on her epaulets together with a feint blue between, walked purposely along the deck towards them.

'Good afternoon again, Miss Lace,' said Mark to the smart and attractive young officer who exuded a certain gravitas and had greeted them on arrival. 'A busy time for the ship's company?'

'Yes, sir, always a great deal to do.'

'Are you on schedule?' asked Kay.

'Absolutely yes, madam, any delay in departure would mean added costs in terms of berthing and pilot fees, compensation to other ships wishing to dock and extra fuel costs in making up lost time to our next destination. And so everyone has to be on their toes. But there's a good team down there,' adding with a confident smile, 'and they always get the job done.'

Faraday looked down again at the quayside. 'A great deal to load on board?'

'Yes. I don't know exactly but there will be about three thousand pounds of fish, twelve thousand pounds of fresh fruit, four thousand pounds of potatoes and,' she paused and said with that engaging smile, 'most importantly, six hundred gallons of ice cream.'

'Ah, thank goodness for that,' said Kay, smiling indulgently, feigning grateful relief. 'My husband will be pleased, he likes his ice-cream with everything,' then asked looking at pallets of eggs, 'and the eggs?'

'Oh, yes. I think it's twenty-seven thousand this time around.'

'Twenty-seven thousand?' said Mark incredulously.

'Oh, yes. Everyone wants an English breakfast or omelettes, and all are vital for our cakes. You see we make everything fresh on the day.'

'So we understand. That's reassuring. Thank you, but we mustn't keep you.'

'Thank you,' she replied and paused. 'It's Mr and Mrs Faraday isn't it?'

'Yes, Miss Lace, and thank you very much for your time.' And she was gone.

Mark turned to Kay. 'Alivia Lace seems to be on the ball,' adding, 'and the Deputy Chief of Security. A useful person to know.'

'And *we* know that *we* are on holiday,' said Kay, raising an eyebrow but knowing that he was hopelessly incorrigible. Although, the truth was, they recognised that they both were.

'Yes, yes,' he said not impatiently. Adding, 'of course,' with little certainty.

They walked a little further along the port-side deck towards the stern. They noticed the security staff with their drug probes and sniffer dogs; the Customs officials; the fork-lift truck drivers eager to move the pallets up the ramp's slight incline to disappear into the bowels of the ship; ship's officers from Housekeeping and Catering, armed with clip boards and radios supervised the loading, some with satisfaction, others waving frantically.

At the dock's security gates trucks were exiting, others awaiting clearance to enter. At the barrier they noticed a black Audi A6 had moved forward behind a lorry. The driver was questioned. Papers were produced. Papers examined. The car was directed forward only to travel about five hundred yards to what appeared to be a staff gangway. A big man in a black suit and wearing dark wrap-around glasses stepped out of the car's front passenger seat and opened the rear door which allowed a man wearing a light grey suit to step out onto the quayside. The light grey suit carried a stainless-steel case in his left hand and shook the hand of the dark suited man. After a very few moments, the Audi swept carefully around and drove towards the barrier as the light grey suit mounted the gangway, nodded to a tall, male security officer and entered the ship. Mark and Kay continued to observe the quayside activity and were as intrigued as they were equally mystified when empty cardboard cartons, flat-packed, emblazoned with large red crosses were taken on board.

Kay and Mark simply nodded to each other. 'Hey,' said Kay with a huge grin. 'We *are* on holiday.'

'I know. Just people watching and admiring the slick operation quayside, although the little Asian man down there caught my eye.'

'Yes, me too,' agreed Kay. 'He seems agitated, no, more anxious.' She smiled at Mark. 'Okay,' she said capitulating, knowing that they were both as bad as each other, 'we are on holiday.' Kay hugged Mark. 'But we can't stop it can we,' she agreed.

'Look at him now as the papers and bags of sugar are checked.'

'The officer isn't intending to cut open the sugar surely?' queried Kay.

'Just the smaller ones I should think,' suggested Mark as they both peered intently.

The officer cut along the top of one bag and inserted a probe, then sealed the small hole with a red coloured patch. He repeated the process again with a larger bag and checked the probe's reading. Satisfied, he sealed the little hole.

'Well,' said Kay, 'the officer is satisfied. The Asian is satisfied, or should I say relieved.'

'I think if you and I were down there we would double-check as the pallets were actually unloaded. Wouldn't you say?'

'I would say that my husband is quite right – as always,' she added with a smile. 'Anyway, let's explore the ship,' said Kay as they walked away checking their *MyWay*, hand-in-hand towards the upper deck.

By now the upper decks were quite crowded with passengers chatting, laughing and drinking whilst awaiting the departure. It was a happy, lively sight. A pleasant time. Below on the quay, most of the empty steel containers had been driven away, pallets collected, as had heaps of cardboard packing and black and yellow bin liners. Fork-lift trucks had trundled away and now mooring lines were being slackened by the line handlers on the quay to be singled up like wet writhing snakes back into the ship. The water between the ship and quayside began to foam as the thrusters and azipods engaged and edged the ship away from the huge black rubber buffers. Passengers began to wave to friends on the shore-side observation platform and sang their version of *'We are Sailing'*. Soon they were sailing past Stanley Park and under the Lionsgate Bridge out into Strait of Georgia 'full away on passage'.

Chapter Three

Sunday, 7th and Monday, 8th April 2019.
Off the coast of Washington and Oregon, United States of America.

SHE WAS BEAUTIFUL. The *Tranquillity* that is. Sleek, painted pure white with two pale green funnels, proceeding at thirteen knots to disturb the sea just a little, the ripples from her bow losing their momentum as they reached the shoreline of Washington State, commonly known as *The Evergreen State* because of its forests and a multitude of State parks.

Their holiday had already taken on a magical air. Everything was perfection. The very first evening on board had been a casual affair with a sumptuous buffet in the *Goodwood* restaurant in contrast to the second evening's more formal dinner - *The Captain's Gala Party.* Everyone dressed for dinner, Mark in a Brook Taverner *Sapphire* dinner suit and Kay looking radiant in a pale green and gold-trimmed Karen Millen creation. The captain, Captain Robert Dunbar, was handsome and charming, and he knew it, as he patiently shook hands with the passengers and photographs were taken in the *Miame Atrium.* It was an irksome chore but he rather liked the attention.

Champagne corks perpetually popped like a gentle artillery barrage and tiny balloons drifted from on high as a pianist at a grand piano played a carefully selected selection of tunes made famous by Richard Clayderman and James Last. Waiters hovered. Waiting. Alert. Others moved skilfully and attentively amongst the passengers. Everyone was full of smiles – except the quite handsome Chief of Security, Andrew Craddock, whose rugged facial expression fluctuated between charming affability to anxious restlessness as if living was a burden. Maybe his official responsibilities were heavy and onerous. Was that it, Kay and Mark wondered?

***

Today, the 7th, Mark and Kay continued to explore *Tranquillity* after their breakfast in the open *Leave Your Worries Behind* restaurant on the After Deck, a reminder of which, if there needed to be one, was the effervescent wake that trailed far behind them. But first they returned to their stateroom and retrieved their life jackets from under their bed and made their way to their muster station in the theatre for the statutory lifeboat drill. It wasn't entirely a serious affair, at least not for all the passengers. Everyone tried on their life jackets with varying degrees of success. Maybe some passengers, even some staff members, thought it amusing or unnecessary and inconvenient. Others appeared a little anxious. Ship's officers were methodical and on stage against a backdrop of diagrams, deck plans and video presentations with junior crew members dressed in orange-coloured tabards emblazoned with large letters in black.

Eventually, directed by an officer on stage with a microphone, various groups shuffled their way out of the theatre, *'The West End'*, to their designated assembly point under a lifeboat that would also act as a tender for shore excursions. There was a stiff breeze and some passengers, after the warmth of the theatre, shivered a little which seemed to concentrate their minds as Mark wrapped Kay, standing immediately in front of him looking out to sea, in his protective arms. Officers checked passengers and staff off their lists, answered questions and reorganised some of the confused. The exercise had lasted about forty minutes at the end of which everyone dispersed to their staterooms, returning the lifejackets under their beds.

Mark and Kay went down to Deck 7 and walked through the dazzling boutique concessions, hovering at the perfumeries, but particularly stopping at *'Jewels just for You from Around the World'* a large circular concession with a central island.

'You seem to be attracted to the emeralds, madam?' said the man in the grey suit whom Mark and Kay had seen at the boat drill. His lapel badge named him as 'GERALD Featherstone', his first name being in the upper case. He looked like a Gerald, perfectly groomed, with a contrasting shirt which matched tie and pocket handkerchief; immaculate fingernails and small delicate hands; maybe very slightly over-weight but with a round smiling face, a person who would be patient and eager to please, although without doubt a handsome commission in mind. He appeared perfect for his role.

'We are keen to buy my wife some jewellery, Mr Featherstone,' said Mark, 'a reminder of this holiday. You have a dazzling display of diamonds,' he continued, distracted for a moment, pointing towards a central island behind Mr Featherstone, a display made all the more magnificent by the overhead lighting.

'A holiday gift, sir, a fine gesture if I may say. The diamonds are splendid. of course, but I do have a small collection of emeralds here,' he said stretching out his hands at his side rather like the inviting embrace of a priest standing before the alter facing his congregation.

Kay smiled a 'thank you'. Mr Featherstone was instantly captivated. For a moment he was speechless, not only at the thought of the commission but of her compelling Oriental beauty and, maybe also, the scent of her *Five Forty* perfume by Kurkdijan, a fragrant combination of jasmine, saffron and cedarwood, ridiculously expensive and not her work-a-day perfume but reserved for special occasions and this voyage. Featherstone felt strangely intimidated by Kay, but this would only be the beginning.

'I understand,' said Mark, bringing Featherstone back to reality, 'that Cartacina De Indias, Colombia and Puntarenas, Costa Rica are famed for them.'

'That is absolutely correct, sir,' recognising Mark's knowledge graciously. 'I have a number of examples on board but have arranged to receive a consignment when we reach Acapulco on the 14th in preparation for a marvellous display before we reach Costa Rica on the 17th . As I say, I do have a small selection over here, madam,' he said smiling as he gestured them toward a glittering display case.

Mark and Kay moved towards the display. Mr Featherstone pondered for a moment as Mark and Kay examined the display of jewels. There was a silence as he considered the potential risk of what he seemed compelled to say. He was emboldened by her beauty and decided that the risk would be worth the anticipated commission and spoke. 'In this time of political correctness, one has to be so very careful not to offend by a genuine observation but, if I may say, madam, your complexion could not be enhanced but would be complimented, if any was needed, by any emerald.'

'Thank you, Mr Featherstone,' said Kay kindly although Mark gave Featherstone a dark look as if he was examining a painting displayed at The Tate Modern and couldn't quite make up his mind if he liked it or not.

For a moment Featherstone sensed danger and thought another offer would be a prudent gesture before Mark had made up his mind and responded. 'I could visit you in your stateroom for a private viewing on the 16th whilst we are at sea. Would that be at all helpful, sir? Madam?'

'That would be nice, Mark, wouldn't it?' said Kay then turned to Featherstone. 'We were considering a necklace and possibly earrings.'

'That would be very helpful, Mr Featherstone,' agreed Mark enthusiastically who had been wanting to buy Kay some jewellery for months and months. 'Would eleven o'clock be good, Mr Featherstone, but for no longer than thirty minutes?'

'Eleven would be perfect, sir, and for thirty minutes,' replied Featherstone without any further consideration – although any time would be good as far Featherstone was concerned if it offered the opportunity for a sale. 'Could I enquire as to your names, please?' he asked.

'Of course, it's Mr and Mrs Mark Faraday,' replied Kay, 'and we are on 9 in 208.'

Featherstone seemed for a moment to fumble with his computer screen. His cheery face became slightly pale. His smile a little set and tense. His heart rate increased. He realised what was happening in his mind and imagined that his facial expression, slight as it might be, reflected his anxious thoughts. He quickly decided that a bogus but plausible explanation for his fumbling was advised.

'Don't you just hate technology, madam,' he said as he began to scratch his head and moved into recovery mode and his smile returned – slightly, although somewhat forced. 'There we are, I have it now, madam. Eleven o'clock on the 16th in Stateroom 208 for a private viewing. Thank you so much and I am confident that I won't disappoint you,' he said directly to Kay.

'I'm sure you won't, Mr Featherstone,' said Kay reassuringly.

They both walked away arm in arm, Kay burying her head into Mark's chest. 'And only thirty minutes?' she queried.

'Yes, I thought so. I don't want to be trapped in an open-ended conversation by a salesman and have to be rude to get rid of him.'

'I agree. Let's just see what he has on offer.' After a few more steps, she said: 'And you noticed his reaction when I gave him our name. He seemed … flustered.'

'Yes, he was a little flustered, partly due to the fact that he has the hots for you.'

'Behave, Mark,' she said hugging him more closely.

'I always behave,' replied Mark with a grin. 'I was purely making an objective observation. Maybe his thoughts of you got all mixed up with his comments about hating technology. The scratching of his head was all part of a *displacement* activity.' As always throughout his career, Mark's degree in psychology was proving useful. 'Nevertheless, if you don't mind would you have Pippa check him out,' said Mark, referring to DI Pippa Blanchard of Special Branch, adding humorously, 'purely out of interest, of course.'

'Of course I don't mind, dear. As you say, *purely out of interest* because we *are* on holiday,' said Kay good heartedly as they wandered off to the *West End* theatre that occupied two decks. But a perceptive Kay was equally interested.

They took their mid-morning Italian coffee in *St Mark's Square* overlooking the *Miame Atrium* whilst a pianist played '*ABBA*' songs, then a snack lunch in *The Globe*, designed as a very English-styled public house, with a wide range of beers and food, including fish and chips; sausages and mash potato; ham and mustard, and beef and horseradish sandwiches.

The bar was arranged in alcoves featuring portraits of British sailors, predominantly explorers, including Sir John Franklin, a map depicting his expeditions in search of the fabled North West Passage which was imposed upon by his portrait and plans of his ships: HMS *Erebus* and HMS *Terror*. He died at the age of 61 in 1847 due to the poisoning of his supplies by poorly preserved tinned food.

Similarly, Captain James Cook's expeditions were portrayed by detailed maps and his ships: HMS *Resolution* and HMS *Endeavour*.

Henry Hudson's ill-fated search for the North West Passage was also illustrated as was a picture of his ship: the *Half Moon*, together with images of Henry, his son and seven of his crew who were cast adrift following a mutiny in 1611 never to be seen again.

Captain Robert Falcon Scott died only twelve miles from his ice-bound depot that would have provided him with his desperately needed food and shelter in 1912. The route of his expedition was illustrated along with the superimposed image of HMS *Discovery* and the octagonal shaped Polar Medal suspended from a pure white ribbon.

Sir Francis Drake also featured with a world map illustrating his many travels and his death near Panama from dysentery, together with his ship, the *Golden Hind*.

Finally, there was Admiral Lord Nelson. There were no maps simply the inspiring portrait by Lemuel Francis Abbott of the admiral wearing his Orders, decorations and his magnificent hat with its Turkish jewel with a feint imposition of a plan of HMS *Victory* in the lower left quarter and a ghost-like portrait of Lady Hamilton in the upper right quarter.

With so many tragedies illustrated it could easily have been that *The Globe* would be a gloomy venue, but not at all. There was a buoyant and cheerful atmosphere, and, if the famous sailors were considered at all by the patrons, it would have probably generated pride in examples of human determination, imagination, fortitude, sacrifice and courage. And the food was good too.

After lunch they descended to the next deck and asked the reception staff if they could peer into both the two main restaurants: the *Ascot* and *Silverstone*. The staff were, of course, very accommodating and took the opportunity to remind Mark and Kay that *Afternoon Tea* could be taken in the *Ascot* at 3.15.

Both restaurants were luxurious in every detail. Not in any way crowded. Again, there appeared to be a relaxed welcoming atmosphere where diners were served by smiling and unobtrusive waiting staff wearing white gloves, eager to advise and please. Clearly, Mark and Kay concluded that *Afternoon Tea* would have to be tested.

The remainder of their day was spent watching a demonstration of the Tango, the origins of which can be discovered in Argentina and spread to North America and Europe. The complex variations were explained by Edmundo Gardel and Nestor Virta. Their demonstrations and the accompanying music were sensual and mesmerising, particularly the *gancho* involving hooking one's leg around one's partner's leg or body. 'I think we should skip that part or I shall probably fall over,' said Mark hardly containing his laughter.

'I think you are right, dear, although we could experiment in our cabin,' said Kay provocatively, a provocation that would be impossible to resist, made all the more so by her perfume, *Five Forty*.

Shortly they returned to their stateroom. They experimented.

***

Later, dinner in the *Silverstone* provided an opportunity for Mark and Kay to people-watch. And there was a lot to watch. Most were enjoying their meals that included *Grilled Smoked Pork Loins Steaks, Canon of Lamb with Red Peppers and Spinach* or *Red Snapper with Papaya Salad* and so much more. Most diners were relaxed, pleased to shed thoughts of their daily lives, maybe some - well quite a few - pretending to be people they were not, whilst others needed to pontificate about how big and successful their businesses were, how they had met members of the Royal family at a Buckingham Palace Garden Party, how clever their children were at their expensive independent schools or how big their lawn mower was!

Mark and Kay had been on a couple of ten- day cruises before and it was why they were more comfortable to dine alone so as to particularly avoid any conversations about parking tickets their fellow diners had received, the failure of the police to arrest a burglar who had broken into a neighbour's home or the recent arrests of ecclesiastical serial sex offenders. But who were they, those who were pretending to be who they were not, their pasts whatever they declared them to be? It always amused Mark and Kay because such inventive pretence was mostly innocent enough, the harmless exaggerated conversations that helped people feel more at ease as they navigated their way through life.

Interesting characters, nevertheless. There was a married couple in their late 50s, she in a motorised wheelchair and he patient and supremely attentive to her every need. There was another couple who, from snippets of conversation, appeared to be doctors and another couple in their mid 40s, the lady of which seemed to giggle at the least provocation and apparently owned a number of children's nurseries. There was a lone elderly lady who appeared identical to that famous actress of years past, Dame Margaret Rutherford, and seemed intrigued and amused by all her fellow passengers, her head held on one side peering about inquisitively. Always seated at or near Table 16 a couple, maybe in their very early forties, heavy in body, neck and face from Eastern Europe, they thought by the name of Heckhausen, spoke little English and, whilst polite and courteous, were anonymous 'grey' people who rarely spoke to any of the other passengers.

Whilst Mark and Kay also tended to keep themselves to themselves too, they were drawn during *Afternoon Tea* to a Mr and Mrs Hewer-Scott from Lincolnshire who owned and ran a number of furniture stores in East Anglia and The Midlands, offering bedroom, lounge and dining room furnishings. A pleasant couple in their late 40s, clearly successful and attractive but without a trace of arrogance simply absorbed in each other's amused company.

But, would Mark and Kay continue to be amused with all the passengers throughout this cruise?

Chapter Four

Tuesday, 9th April 2019.
San Francisco, United States of America.

DURING BREAKFAST Mark and Kay were distracted or was it intently focused. In their stateroom they had access to news on their TV but the ship also printed a daily newspaper. Newspapers had once always been a familiar and comforting feature of cruises, but not so much now with instant, up-to-date news via TV. Some cruise lines didn't produce a newspaper, maybe just a few briefing sheets, but the *Tranquillity* did produce a newspaper, the *Tranquil News*, because the British liked their daily paper. Papers were useful. The paper gave details of the ship's daily events, their timings and locations; the full range of entertainment in the morning, afternoon and evening; details of key members of the crew; the history and maps of the ports soon to be visited and also world-wide news, including that of the UK.

One such news item referred to Beachy Head, the chalk headland in East Sussex, England near Eastbourne, overlooking the English Channel and providing for panoramic views towards the Isle of Wight. The white chalk cliffs towered five hundred and thirty-one feet above the shingle beach on which was actually built the now much photographed red and white lighthouse. The first lighthouse was built on the nearby cliffs but, because of the low cloud, the light was very often obscured and so a new lighthouse was built in 1831 on the beach itself and had since attracted thousands of curious visitors annually. The cliffs also attracted those with suicidal tendencies. In fact, amazingly, Beachy Head is rated the third most common place on planet Earth for suicides!

Page three of the ship's newspaper featured, below the crease, a photograph of Beachy Head and the dramatic shattered remains of a silver-grey Range Rover Vogue on the beach. The photograph was overlaid with measurements and the assumed route of the vehicle had taken indicated by a series of white dashes. The 'accident' had apparently occurred during the night of the 5th April. The deceased driver had not been named. The local Sussex police were investigating but declined to comment further at this stage saying that enquiries were 'on going'. One 'local source' cautiously speculated that a suggestion had been made that the recent success of the National Crime Agency and UK Board Force agents may have been linked to the incident. Further details of the number of annual suicides at Beachy Head were included in the article together with the nationalities, age and gender of those who had died.

One member of the ship's crew had also read the article. He was worried. He had reason to be worried. Very worried. In fact paranoid. He was sure that there would be a link with him and the recent success of the NCA – a deadly link.

***

They had assembled in *'The West End'*. When the number of their coach had been called, Mark and Kay had made their way through to their disembarkation station and their air-conditioned coaches waiting on the quayside.

There is a lively expectation with most shore excursions, but with San Francisco, as with New York, Paris, Sydney, Rome and London, there was an air of considerable excitement too. And San Francisco didn't disappoint. The tour took a route to North Beach and the Colt Tower which had featured prominently in the *'Dirty Harry'* police movies, as Lawrence, 'but please call me "Larry"', Hartnall, their courier was delighted to point out. Then on to Nob Hill, Haight and Richmond, to cross the iconic Bay Bridge and coffee at Vista Point North. A snack lunch was taken at North Beach at the renowned *Mama's* on Filbert and Stockton where pancakes were delicious and described 'as light as a feather'. A trolley bus ride was a must, from Powell and Market to Beach and Hyde via Washington and Jackson.

The coach route ensured excellent views of the abandoned but sinister island prison of Alcatraz, once home to the notorious gangster, Al Capone. Passengers were pleased that the coach stopped allowing them an opportunity for photographs with Alcatraz as a backdrop which seems to particularly amuse an expensively dressed, powerfully built man accompanied by a young, trim figured blond lady who answered to the name 'Destiny'. The man had the handsome chiselled features of a movie star although the set of his mouth caught Kay's attention, a sort of malevolent half-smile, whilst Destiny was by any measure an attractive woman but in a cheap 1950s Hollywood star way.

'You are people watching again,' said Kay to Mark. 'You've noticed that pair?'

'Of course,' she confirmed. 'Destiny is determined to have a good holiday, but he's … '

'Furtive?' offered Mark.

'Yes, I would say so. There's a tinge of arrogance about him. Smug to be viewed as attractive to many women I should think and to have a beautiful woman on his arm, but shifty don't you think?' suggested Kay.

'Yes, and he's not always relaxed is he? I've noticed him in the restaurant and when we are in port. He's someone else who intrigues me,' Mark said. 'Just wondering who he might be, that's all.'

As the coach continued its journey, it passed the impressive City Hall on McAllister, a building that would not have looked out of place in any capital of the world, but it was in stark contrast with the queues of the poor awaiting state relief and guarding their 'requisitioned' supermarket trollies, trollies which were twice the size of a British counterpart and which were able to be converted effectively into their homes as the nights drew in. This sight prompted Larry to explain the cardboard boxes that some passengers had noted being taken ashore every time the *Tranquillity* docked.

'I've been asked about the brown cardboard boxes with red crosses,' said Larry, 'crosses like the cross of St George, that are unloaded when we dock. Well, they are all part of the pet project of your Chief of Security. Inside the cardboard boxes are insulated ice boxes containing food. Not contaminated food, I hasten to add,' he said quickly. 'Waste food is composted but food that is nearing its 'best-before' date is given to the poor. The chefs estimate how much food we will be consumed, of course,' he added reasonably, 'and which dishes will be popular, but tastes vary on every cruise and they don't always get it just right. They dare not risk using food that would be near the 'best-before' date, and so, there are port-side arrangements and the food is distributed to the Salvation Army, soup kitchens, night shelters and food banks. I can tell you,' he added with a smile, 'some of the poor folk in this town will enjoy fine dining tonight.' There were murmurs of approval and some clapping, even nodding as if the passengers should be congratulating themselves!

As they continued their tour, Kay leaned into Mark. He lowered his head. 'The figures don't add up. We could check the maths again tonight, don't you think?

Chapter Five

Wednesday, 10th April 2019.
Off the coast of the Santa Lucia Range, United States of America.

AFTER BREAKFAST, Mark and Kay explored more of the ship before a not too energetic jog twice around the ship, a total of a half-mile, and then a work-out in the gym.

They freshened up and changed then relaxed on the Sun Deck. There they saw Alivia Lace in pristine whites with her assistant. He was quite short. Shorter than Miss Lace, but equally smart in turn-out with two gold bars on his epaulettes, more to provide a reassuring indication of authority for passengers and an element of equality with customs and police officials than actual weight of responsibility. He was maybe three or four years younger than Miss Lace. His body language appeared indicative of him as a person. His personality would have been shaped by his background, experiences and culture, and thus possibly more comfortable in a submissive position yet possessing an ego requiring authority. He nodded respectfully as she spoke. He smiled but said little. He appeared at ease to agree, responding to requests or orders. Not a challenger but maybe there was little to question. An unreflective and unimaginative subordinate maybe thought Mark, his university studies and years of service inevitably bobbing to the surface and prompting his thoughts. As Assistant Chief Robert Pitman, for it was whom he transpired to be, wandered off towards the prow, Mark and Kay almost instinctively moved together and spoke, as if casually and by chance, to Miss Lace.

'Not quite so hectic for you today?' asked Mark, a question designed to be exploratory. One that encouraged a response. There was a short moment of hesitation as if she was unsure of her reply. She glanced at her watch, then to her left, then to her right.

'If you wait a few minutes, sir, you might be pleasantly surprised as to how hectic it can be as well as reassured,' she said, maybe as an instinctive test of trust.

Mark and Kay looked at each other, bemused. 'Reassured you say?' queried Mark.

'Just a few more minutes, sir,' said Miss Lace hoping to add a little excitement with a conspiratorial smile. They waited four minutes, at which time there followed three prolonged masthead blasts on the ship's horn and the announcement: 'Man overboard.'

A life-sized mannequin dummy had already been heaved into the water from the port-side for'ard chain locker. In response to the 'man overboard' announcement an orange flare was now fired from the bridge into the sea by a young Fourth Deck Officer, clearly taken by surprise by this sudden and completely unexpected responsibility thrust upon him. The response from the ship was almost immediate as she turned to port so that her churning propellors would avoid the dummy. Derricks rumbled. Mark and Kay peered over the side. The rescue RIB was winched out from the side of the ship, not too far, but far enough to allow the rescue crew to clamber aboard.

The RIB was lowered as the crew checked again to ensure that their personal kit was secure. The RIB hovered above the waves as the *Tranquillity* reduced speed and executed a 'Williamson Turn' to bring the ship back to the point it had previously turned through, although tides and currents would have to be taken into account and the numbers calculated by the bridge computers.

It took what seemed a lifetime for the 43,000 tonne ship to reduce her speed sufficiently to allow the RIB to be safely dropped into the sea. But once she had done so the RIB with its three-man crew sped off towards the orange flare at 32 knots whilst two of the tenders were already being prepared to assume a 'structured search and rescue' role by which time the bridge had already announced reassuringly that this was an on-going exercise.

As they watched, they talked. Finally Mark commented: 'Very impressive, Miss Lace, but it still took forty-three minutes to make the recovery,' he said at the same time raising his hand, 'not a criticism, I assure you, but the sea is relatively calm and still very cold, just glad that I haven't fallen in the sea off the Aleutian Islands,' said Mark referring to the islands situated off the coast of Alaska.

'You are absolutely right, Mr Faraday,' she replied with a smile, nodding in agreement. 'The sea temperature here is about 13⬚. In ordinary clothing you would be fortunate to last more than an hour.'

'Well, darling,' he said to Kay laughing and hugging is wife, 'you better not push me over.' He turned to Alivia Lace. 'Anyway, altogether very interesting, Miss Lace. Thank you for giving us the heads-up.'

Miss Lace probably should not have given them the heads-up at all. But, for some reason, she had trusted them then and into the future not to gossip and this seemed a good time to gently probe.

'You interest me, Miss Lace,' said Kay. 'You carry your uniform well, if I may say, and your walk is elegant but with a certain military, how shall I put it … style.'

'You are very perceptive, madam. My father is in the army and my school had an Officer Training Corps, but I found it all a little too restrictive, so I joined a bank but found that to be too boring seated behind a glass screen for most of the day. My father introduced me to a military policeman who,' she added with an open modestly, 'smoothed my way on board.'

'And you don't find this role too restrictive or boring?' asked Kay.

'Oh, no. It's rather like working in a very pleasant, vibrant and interesting modern town. There's surprisingly quite a good deal to do but I also have a lot of freedom. I'm really happy. I share a cabin with a very nice girl, a junior navigator, and I'm seeing the world – and not from the back of an army truck.'

'We seem to be constantly taking up your time, Miss Lace. But thank you.'

'It's not a problem,' she said, seemingly not eager to break off the conversation. 'My job is often about rosters but I think it should be mostly about people. Observing people, particularly listening to what people have to say. Speaking with them.'

There was no point in pressing this attractive person further, not for the moment at least. Miss Lace would come to them, they were sure. 'That must always be so and we've enjoyed speaking with you, Miss Lace,' said Mark. 'Maybe we could continue our conversation another time, say during *Afternoon Tea* if you are free of course.'

'I'm usually free between 3.30 and 3.45. I will look out for you,' she said with an encouraging smile.

Kay and Mark pondered the substance of her reply. Was it a proposal they wondered?

***

Mark and Kay returned to their stateroom – a beautifully appointed junior suite which included a splendid bedroom and bathroom area with a lounge mid-way and through the floor-to-ceiling glass sliding doors to their balcony. Their steward, Seselija, from the Solomon Islands was there.

'I later time come back, sir,' he said apologetically.

'No. No, it's okay, we are only picking up a few things.' Mark and Kay collected their books, Mark a jumper and Kay a gilet. Mark spoke. 'You always seem to be working. Out of interest, how many staterooms do you look after?'

'Eleven, sir, and five officer cabin.'

'And your cabin is on Deck 3 or 4 I think which you share?'

'Deck 3 with three other steward.'

'And how big is your cabin?'

'About size same,' he replied indicating an area about the size of Mark and Kay's lounge.

'It must be cramped for you?'

'All crew cabin same. Officer, they have single cabin or with one other officer but we share with three other. I not mind, sir, we all the good friend.'

'And how long have you worked for the company?'

'Nine year.'

'And you are able to send money home?'

'Yes, sir. For my mother and for help my children the education.'

'You have photographs?'

He smiled, pleased that an interest was being shown. He pulled a brown leather wallet from his trouser pocket and pointed at a photograph it contained. 'This my wife, Juanita, and my son, Jaime, and my daughter, Adalia.'

'They must be very proud of you?'

'That I hope, but it is Seselija,' he said holding his hands to his chest, 'who very proud of them also.'

***

'Craddock,' answered Craddock as he held his cabin's phone in his hand.

'Just listen,' said a reasonably cultured but no-nonsense English voice with a Celtic lilt. 'You don't know me but I know you. I know what the red crossed boxes are for.'

Craddock froze. He hadn't expected such a call. 'So listen in. The consignments have doubled.'

'What do you mean,' he protested in a panic-ridden voice. 'I can't just do that?' although he did not question the instruction. He had been warned that a 'minder' or 'enforcer' would sometimes travel on the ship.

'Are you hard of hearing or just utterly stupid? You can and you will. If you don't then it won't just be Beachy Head the passengers will be talking about, it will be you. Make sure there are no loose ends.'

'Don't threaten me, I'm …. ,' blustered Craddock but his remark was cut short.

'If you can't do your job, then I will have to do mine.'

'Who are you?'

'I'm the person who is everywhere and nowhere on this ship, Mr Craddock, and I will put you over the side if you fail.'

The line went dead. An ominous, over-whelming, dark, oppressive silence filled Craddock's cabin as he sank onto his bed. He leant forward, head in his hands.

***

That evening, Mark and Kay ate early so that they would be ready for the second performance of the evenings' entertainment, but during their joint choice of the main course, *Pampiette of Beef*, they noticed the absence of the Chief of Security who very often dined in the *Silverstone*.

They glanced about and could see an agitated Craddock near the entrance foyer to the restaurant apparently using his ship's pager. 'He's paging Pitman,' observed Kay as Assistant Chief Pitman, seated on a distant table, fumbled for his pager under his napkin. He seemed to finger a reply and then excused himself with a certain degree of urgency from his table with an apologetic and reassuring smile to his fellow diners. When Mark and Kay looked towards the foyer, Craddock was nowhere to be seen.

Chapter Six

Thursday, 11th April 2019.
At sea, west of Punta Eugenia, Mexico.

THE EARLY MORNING TELEVISION NEWS had details of the Beachy Head victim, named as Nicolas Peskov. The local police had now bumped his death up to 'suspicious'. Mark opened their stateroom door and removed the daily paper from the clear glass rack, made coffee for them both and sat on their balcony in the white dressing gown embroidered in gold with the ship's crest. The paper contained more details of Peskov, but now on the front page above the crease, a man who had been on trial the previous year at Canterbury Crown Court in connection with the importation of drugs from Belgium to the UK but was acquitted.

'This information would have come in last evening,' speculated Mark as he was joined by Kay, 'and given the on-board printers just enough time to include it in today's paper.'

'At about the same time that Craddock and Pitman were hopping about, wouldn't you say?' Kay suggested in a hushed voice, her arms around his neck.

'Maybe,' speculated Mark. 'They could have been responding to all manner of events, but, if they were

responding to the news about Peskov, why should they?'
What has Peskov got to do with this ship?'

'You have reservations about Craddock?'

'Craddock's a showman. A presentable showman – when he thinks he's on show - but there's every indication that he's a worrier too, burdened down, preoccupied,' suggested Mark. He paused as Kay sat down, poured more coffee and opened the little caddy of biscuits. 'He has an important job with a range of responsibilities, no doubt, although essentially routine, but Lace and Pitman seem to take everything in their stride. He doesn't.'

'But they aren't sat in the "buck stops here chair",' observed Kay reasonably.

Mark remained silent. Thinking. He didn't reply immediately. But what Kay had said was quite correct. 'That's very true,' he agreed after a few moments. 'I know, I know, but he seems to have a good team of uniformed security people, ex-Gurkhas, all of whom have a reputation for hard work, competency and reliability. Okay, they will be busy. There will always be pilfering by staff and even thefts from passengers. However well-regulated a ship is there will always be too many temptations. There will be drug issues and domestic problems amongst the passengers themselves who thought a cruise would sort out their problems only to find that the cruise reminded them of what they had been missing or the close confines of their cabin only tending to magnify their problems.'

Mark was quiet for a few short moments more then spoke again. 'I'm probably not being fair, but there's an anxiety about him at specific times, maybe there's a pattern there, yet there is very unlikely to be a petrol bomb throwing riot on board and we are not sailing in waters where there is known to be piracy.'

'Well, I agree that there's something about Craddock that makes us both feel uncomfortable,' said Kay lightly, 'and Alivia Lace might say something of interest.'

Deputy Chief of Security Lace could, but she would not reveal that Craddock was often confined to his cabin on a restricted diet of chicken gruel, bread and a banana after vomiting due to stress. Well, not yet anyway.

'Golf 122419', announced the tannoy quietly but clearly.

***

They had lunch on the After Deck before going to *'The West End'* to view the demonstration of the Rumba by Edmundo and Nestor which was amusing and exciting, against a background of songs including: *'Wish I was your Lover'* by Enrique Iglesias, *'Besame Muncho'* by Andrea Bocelli and *'Como Me Duele Perdecte'* by Gloria Estefan. Passengers were invited to participate, something that was very entertaining for the spectator although daunting for those daring passengers prepared to participate.

With its origins in northern Cuba, essentially a Rumba is associated with exciting parties, the dance is particularly noted for its side-to-side hip movements which Nestor explained with a series of remarkably subtle and intimate demonstrations of two renditions of the Rumba: the *yabu* and the *guaguanco*, the latter being particularly provocative and flirtatious with the man being aggressively sensual and the woman defensive.

'As you are 6-4 and I am 5-3, the hip-to-hip business is likely to be tricky,' purred Kay provocatively as she moved closer to her lover and gently forced her left leg between Mark's legs.

'Unless the partners are lying down, don't you think?' suggested a grinning Mark.

'Isn't that amazing, darling. I've been imagining exactly the same thing,' said Kay with a wicked smile. 'Lying down would be the best so that the man could become, maybe, less aggressive and the woman less defensive. What do you think?'

'Yes, this is clearly a very important issue and I've been thinking along those line too,' said Mark with mock seriousness. 'Harmony is the thing and, as there's a bit of a swell out there, I would hate it if we fell off the bed at a critical moment.'

'Only one critical moment?' corrected Kay.

Chapter Seven

Friday, 12th April 2019.
Cabo San Lucas, Mexico.

THEY BERTHED. The dock-side activities commenced at a little after 9am once the *Tranquillity* had been made fast. Mark and Kay remained on board, on their balcony, Mark reading Roger Hill's *'Destroyer Captain'* and Kay reading *'The Sun is my Undoing'* by Marguerite Steen. They had seen Craddock on the quayside, strutting about immaculately dressed as always but rather officiously, seemingly paying more attention to the arrival of trucks than anything else, yet making a point of waving in a friendly and nonchalant manner to departing coaches. Was this a *displacement* activity wondered Mark as he made some more coffee only to be interrupted by Kay.

'It's "go" time, darling,' called Kay.

Both Kay and Mark resumed their balcony seats and shuffled them forward to see Craddock take on a role akin to a traffic warden directing a grey, unmarked panel truck to a coned-off bay. He spoke to the driver and then returned to the ship to re-emerge with two kitchen staff carrying a brown cardboard box with red crosses. This was loaded on to the truck and exchanged for four flat packs before driving off down the length of the quay to the dock gates. One of the kitchen staff appeared to offer to carry the flat packs but this Craddock seemed to decline. Craddock didn't resume his strutting. He milled about as if unperturbed, yet he had taken charge of the flat packs, then took them up the ramp and into the bowels of the ship.

'Interesting pantomime,' said Mark as they shuffled their chairs back towards the balcony doors.

'I agree,' replied Kay. 'Why didn't he just call up the porters and get them to bring the box out?

'And why did he take charge of the flat packs. That wasn't the task for a security chief?'

'And why did it take him, what was it, seventeen minutes to bring out the box. Surely the box would have been ready to hand, in an orderly pre-determined sequence ready for off-loading?' queried Kay.

'It's the maths that bugging me again,' said Mark. 'Why four flat pack boxes. They can't possibly have to get rid of four boxes of food when we will only be at sea for a day.'

'Maybe it's all about 'best before' dates and the needs of the poor who live near particular ports and the distribution arrangements.'

'That could be the case, but you don't believe that?' queried Mark.

'Of course not,' she replied. 'Craddock is up to something, maybe a little racket on the side, like the inn keeper of *Les Misérables*. Maybe something more. I'm sure it will be more, much more.' She shook her head from side to side, acknowledging how often people, even those with all the apparent comforts of life, can be so foolish and dishonest, greedy and corrupt. They exchanged smiles of understanding. 'You know what I'm thinking. It never ceases to intrigue me.'

'I know, but we still find it baffling,' said Mark casually in a relaxed conversational way. 'What is it with human beings?'

'We know,' pondered Kay, 'animals in the wild concentrate in the main on eating and procreating and a lot of sleeping thrown in, whilst humans are also driven by ego, pride, status and ambition.'

'And worryingly, envy and self-interest, bitterness and revenge,' added Mark.

'You're right, of course.' She thought for a long moment. 'I suppose it's a necessary and unattractive ingredient of evolution without which there would be no forward thinking, no imagination, no progress.' She hugged Mark. 'Anyway, on that depressing note, I think we should make progress towards lunch.'

They walked along the deck, hand-in-hand, but Mark was silent. Kay slowed her pace and guided him to the highly varnished wooden handrail. 'What are you thinking?'

'Just a thought. Who looks after the red crossed boxes when Craddock isn't about?'

***

They had their lunch on the After Deck from self-service, in the sunshine with a view towards the lush mountains and clear blue sky. The ship's photographers were out in force, on the quayside waiting for the returning passengers or around the ship. In the Atrium Mark and Kay declined a request from a photographer but agreed to an appointment for a posed photograph during the evening on the sweeping stairs of the *Miame Atrium*.

During *Afternoon Tea*, Mark and Kay sat with a Mr and Mrs David Read.

'Did you hear about Miss Scammel, my dear?' Mrs Read asked Kay as she peered over half-rimmed glasses.

'Miss Scammel? I don't believe I have,' replied Kay.

'Oh, well you see it was Miss Scammel, yesterday morning,' explained Mrs Read, a retired headmistress who always dressed in a combination of black and white, together with black and white earrings, necklaces and hair clips, and even carried an elegant black and white cane.

She spoke to everyone slowly in a slightly high-pitched voice as if she was talking to a rather dim child, 'Miss Scammel took a tumble down the stairs. She eighty-three you know. Eighty-three. Tripped. Went right down. Bump. Only three steps mind you. But three steps it was. The medical people came. Very promptly. Apparently, they answered some sort of coded announcement. Miss Scammel is back in her stateroom now with her lady companion. Nothing broken. Thank goodness. Soon be up and about. Fit as a fiddle. Resilience. And no fuss. That's what it's all about. Resilience and no fuss, my dear.'

'It's reassuring to know that help was readily to hand, Mrs Read,' remarked Kay.

'Oh, yes,' replied a mildly pompous Mrs Read knowingly, 'they are very good on this ship,' adding unnecessarily, 'We've sailed with this line before, of course. They have coded messages, I'm told, for the security, medical and fire people too.'

After tea Mark and Kay attended the port lecture in the theatre. A significant number of passengers had already booked the excursion in Acapulco and this second presentation was for the final places on the coaches.

'Interesting but I don't think so, do you?' said Mark to Kay raising an eyebrow.

'Even with all the precautions in place,' suggested Kay, 'I think the risks are unacceptable.'

Mark and Kay were referring to recent killings by the cartels and city gangs. Once the playground of international figures such as Brigitte Bardot, Elizabeth Taylor and Frank Sinatra, the killings and kidnappings by drug cartels and city gangs had seen the popularity of Acapulco dwindle. Mass killings since 2014 with gun battles and headless corpses in the main streets and tourist area resulted in the city gaining the dubious title of the seventh most deadly city in the world. The role of the local civilian police force had been diminished and the national army taking control in 2018 on the sound reasoning that its soldiers and their families, on rotation from elsewhere far away, were less likely to be intimidated by the local wing of the cartels.

The decision not to go ashore was a disappointment as Mark and Kay were both keen to see the famous *La Quebrada* cliff divers and visit the Fort of San Diego, built in the seventieth century by the Spanish, pentagon in design, to protect against pirates, and renovated to the highest standards with very fine exhibitions. But no, Mark and Kay considered it was a 'risk too far'.

But no worries. Along with deck sports and beauty salons, port lectures and the cinemas, there was always something to do on board including 'get togethers' for groups such as Probus and the Women's Institute, Veteran Associations and Lions International, Rotary and the Freemasons. Faraday wouldn't attend the Freemasons Reunion. He wasn't against freemasonry as such. He acknowledged their tremendous range of charity work and massive funding for good causes including, apparently some fifty percent of the Royal National Lifeboat Institution annual budget. In fact, Faraday had been a Mason but, when he was an Inspector serving in the St Pauls area of Bristol he had been approached by a Mason from another lodge, a property developer, who complained that two of Mark's officers had been less than sufficiently diligent in taking action against a suspected drug user who occupied a flat in one of his properties. The complaint was a complete nonsense and had been made in the hope that a West Indian occupant would be intimidated by the police enquiries and vacate the flat. The developer had lied. His lies could have jeopardised the young officers' careers and potentially created tensions within the community. He had lied in the hope of driving out a black tenant so as to be free to renovate the whole property and complete the whole development with a fine profit. Mark was not prepared to place himself in a compromising position and had since that time never again attended a lodge meeting – but he knew all the secret signs, all the signals, all the words of introduction and acknowledgement.

***

Dinner later that day was excellent and taken against the background of superb Mariachi music performed by a Mexican trio of guitar musicians. The menu consisted of the usual varied options including beef or venison, partridge or turkey, cod or lobster, in fact, anything else a passenger might desire or demand from the chef's inspired and imaginative menus. The evening entertainment was provided by the celebrated guitarist Salome Ruiz followed by Martin Tempest, a hypnotist. All the passenger participants appeared to be selected at random by Martin.

It was a fascinating performance, as fascinating as some passengers found Kay's appearance to be. She wore a broad vertically stripped black and gold full length skirt with a neat gold coloured jacket by Vanessa Seward. She looked, as always, stunning, poised and elegant, full of sophistication. She attracted many glances, some of envy, some of admiration. Few would have assumed that she was the astute head of Special Branch in her force.

They finished their evening in the *Venetian Bar* with a 'Flaming Coffee', an infamous but popular Mexican combination of *Tequila*, *Kahlua* liqueur, *Cinnamon* cream and *Chantilly*. When blue flames rose from this combustible concoction there followed excited and raucous applause from guests and a delighted and wide smile from Paulo Montoya, the bar tender.

Chapter Eight

Saturday, 13th April 2019.
At sea west of the Sierra Madre del Sur, Mexico.

IT WAS ALL BASED UPON FEAR. Everyone in the organisation was fearful of failure. Failure would result in a variety of imaginative, or unimaginable, hideous penalties. Recently, a two-year old child had been dropped into a boiling fish fryer to punish and then encourage the parents to cooperate. And so Craddock was fearful. So also the caller. There would be consequences for him too if he failed to ensure that Craddock carried out his task. He made another call.

'Craddock,' answered the Chief of Security.

'Just a reminder, Craddock. We are in Acapulco tomorrow. The consignment is doubled. It will be waiting for you. Just do it. Don't join the "Fuck Up Club".'

***

The visitors to the Photo and Video Gallery were milling about seeking their photographs. There were thousands to choose from, some taken during shore excursions or in the restaurants, on the Sun Deck or with Captain Robert Dunbar. Many passengers were clearly delighted with their photographs, others not so, whilst others found it amusing to see the less flattering photographs of fellow passengers with one elderly passenger remarking rather too loudly:

'Bloody hell. He fell from the ugly tree'.

'Clifford, for Heaven's sake, decorum please,' chastised, Vera, his wife.

Mark and Kay selected a photograph of them standing against the background of the After Deck and another with them both on the stairs in the *Miame Atrium*. They were a photogenic couple, Kay looking utterly captivating and radiant, with Mark looking smart and proud to be standing at her side. Kay checked her watch. They returned to the stateroom. It would be just before 16:00 GMT when she called DI Pippa Blanchard from their lounge.

Pippa and Kay spoke about domestic and police matters for a few minutes before dealing with the main purpose of the call. 'Two things. Can you take these on? I'm not sure of your operational commitments at the moment so tell me if you can't,' she asked, although she knew what Pippa's answer would be, particularly as Pippa knew that Mark and Kay would not abuse their friendship.

'Of course, just tell me what you want me to do.'

'Okay, see what you can discover about the ship's Chief of Security, a guy by the name of Andrew Craddock and also a jeweller by the name of Gerald Featherstone. He runs an impressive jewellery concession on board. When I gave him our names it seemed to spook him for a moment. He might be a Bristolian or live in Bristol and might have seen Mark or me on TV. It might be nothing, of course.'

'Ah, I see what's going on,' teased Pippa. 'Buying jewels then, are we?'

'Yes, I think so, just as a modest memento of this holiday.'

'No. No,' protested Pippa without a trace of envy. 'Modest? You know that Mark just can't do modest with you.'

***

They took *Afternoon Tea* in the *Ascot* restaurant. Deputy Chief of Security, Alivia Lace, entered the restaurant, glanced around, then made a beeline for Mark and Kay. Mark rose from his chair as Alivia took a seat and was almost immediately attended by a waitress who approached carrying a cup, saucer, plate and napkin.

'Would you care for tea, madame?'

'Thank you, Mary, just tea please,' said Alivia in a genuine manner, not one of an arrogant officer being dismissive of a waitress.

'We can't tempt you with a cake, Miss Lace?' asked Kay.

'Maybe just one,' she said and learnt forward and took a *bichon* from the second tier of the stand.

'I was told that a Miss Scammel had a tumble and we saw you rushing along with the doctor earlier,' said Mark. 'Nothing too serious I hope?' an apparently innocent question that provided an opportunity for Miss Lace to reply.

'Nothing serious,' she replied, keen to ensure that there would be no safety criticisms of the ship. 'I'm told that Miss Scammel apparently lost her grip on the handrail.'

'And I haven't seen your boss about today?' observed Kay.

'He's unwell again. Nothing to do with the food on board but he seems to get tummy problems every now and again. He'll be okay by tomorrow, I'm sure.'

'And I saw you in the multi-gym,' said Kay avoiding any further reference to Craddock, 'it must be so difficult to avoid all this tempting food?'

Alivia Lace fingered her wristwatch which included a *StepsApp* . 'It's surprising how far I walk every day and I am careful with my diet. The food is enticing, and I have to resist.' Once she had drunk her tea she stood to leave. Mark stood too. 'I must go. Maybe we can make this a regular thing?'

'I hope so,' replied Kay who remained silent until Alivia had gone, then asked: 'Why did she come across to us. Am I reading too much into someone simply wanting to rest her feet and have a cup of tea?'

'She wanted to speak with people she thought were semi-sensible,' he replied amusingly, 'and after a diligent search we were the only ones she could find,' then continued more seriously, 'people with whom she could relax for a few moments, people she might wish to trust and bounce thoughts off. If she smells a rat with Craddock for example, who would she feel confident to trust?'

As they left the restaurant, they saw Gerald Featherstone enjoying his tea. He nodded to them both rising from his seat just a little in acknowledgement. He smiled, not a leer but a look as if bewitched. The Faradays nodded in return. 'Well,' whispered Mark, 'that smile was not for me. I think that seeing you has just made his day.'

Chapter Nine

Sunday, 14th April 2019.
Acapulco, Mexico.

THE CHIEF OF SECURITY, Andrew Craddock, occupied a single inside stateroom, whilst Robert Pitman, the Assistant Chief of Security, occupied an inside twin berth stateroom with Martin Ford, the Deputy Purser, as did Ruben De Gennard, the Executive Housekeeper and Dan Davidson, the Third Engineer. Managers of concessions occupied single or twin inside staterooms.

Gerald Featherstone preferred to pay a supplement for single occupancy on account of his schedules, essentially mid-mornings and very late evenings. Captain Robert Dunbar was an exception and had the luxury of an outside balcony stateroom, adapted for his use and for'ard, close to the bridge.

All enjoyed the services of a steward. It was hard work for the stewards. Some passengers tided before they went to breakfast, others left a complete mess. Some passengers, in fact many of them, were demanding and required very speedy attention to their every whim whilst others expected errands to be run, for example, searching for and exchanging books from the library, even going ashore.

Stewards tended to be tolerant and understanding, and also willing. Of course, there was very likely to be tips which were always welcomed, a proportion of which would find their way to their families. Today one of the stewards had been given an envelope with instructions to go ashore at a specific time and visit a café situated in a specific street.

He had followed the instructions and waited in a side street a little while so as to arrive at the café at precisely three o'clock as instructed. It was a scruffy establishment with lounging equally scruffy clientele and filthy white plastic chairs. The owner, Luis Cabrera, although this was probably not his real name, was waiting for him with a rather unnerving toothy grin that would have been similar to that of a sinister Mexican bandit in an old John Wayne movie. Cabrera invited the steward to take one of the filthy white plastic chairs and gave him a glass of iced *pulque*, then went into a back room which he euphemistically described as 'my office'. There he opened the envelope and counted the US dollar bills. He read the pencilled note which was also with the money:

'Make sure he doesn't get back on the ship'.

Cabrera thumbed the bills then stuffed them in to his inside not-so-white jacket pocket. He thought that two hundred dollars was a very generous fee. He would have done the job for much, much less.

***

All the ramps had been removed with the exception of one. It was now six o'clock. Departure had been scheduled for five-thirty. All passengers and crew had returned on board with the exception of one steward. Enquiries had been made with Housekeeping and the Personnel Department to ascertain any previous absences and reasons, but he had an excellent work record. Fellow stewards were tasked to make discreet searches. Enquiries were made of the Medical Centre. But the Italian steward, Fransesco Maresca, could not be found. The hard, realistic truth was that if the delayed crew member had been the Chief Engineer, then Captain Dunbar would have delayed a little longer, but the absence of one steward could not be allowed to jeopardise the sailing any longer. Messages and contact details were left with the port authorities. At six-thirty, Captain Dunbar ordered his ship to let go her lines and make passage for Huatulco.

Chapter Ten

Monday, 15th April 2019.
Huatulco, Mexico.

THE *TRANQUILLITY* WAS ABLE TO DOCK at La Crucecita, the only quay capable of accommodating a cruise liner in this idyllic part of the Mexican state of Oaxaca. Here the tourist industry had steadily developed around nine beautiful white sandy beaches that offered superb opportunities for surfing and scuba diving in the cobalt blue sea as well as being an area where there was an effective programme of conservation of its natural habitat and resources, all protected from further development. Famed for its wide range of traditional fish foods and with an architectural history stretching back two and a half thousand years, it was an idyllic place in stark contrast to Acapulco.

Passengers descended on Huatulco and so there was much less activity on board ship, with little enthusiasm for water volleyball and ping pong tournaments, both of which had to be rescheduled. As with many passengers, Mark and Kay thoroughly enjoyed this relaxed visit. Clearly there was no need for red crossed boxes and this lack of clandestine activity was indicated by the appearance of a remarkably relaxed Craddock on the quayside.

After a quite energetic walking visit, Mark and Kay enjoyed an excellent dinner, *Sautéed Breast of Chicken on Leek and Truffles Macaroni and Crayfish Cream* for Kay and *Suprême of Duck with Grand Marnier and Orange Sauce* for Mark, before visiting a 'Fragrance Event' staged by Chanel and then retiring early to their stateroom. As they made way to Number 208, there was a discreet announcement: 'Bravo 1228134'.

Mark and Kay had already worked out the rudimentary but sensible code system. The announcements were in a code so as not to alarm the passengers. The previous announcement prefixed by 'Golf' indicated 'G' for green, that was for medics. 'Bravo' would be blue, that would be for police or security and 'Romeo' would be red for fire-fighting services. The two digits would indicate the designated unit's call sign and '2' would mean 'go to' a particular location.

Ever inquisitive, Mark and Kay made their way as nonchalantly as they were capable to Deck 8 and Stateroom 134. As they approached, they could see Assistant Chief Pitman and two security staff near 134. The distressed young lady with an hour-glass figure stormed passed them towards the lifts and adjacent ladies' cloakroom. Without speaking with Kay, Mark walked to the left and stood by the lifts, apparently disinterested, and pressed some buttons. The lift doors opened. Two passengers stepped out. Mark stepped in. Kay veered to the right and casually followed the young lady into the ladies' cloakroom just in time to see her vomit into the wash basins and down the front of her blouse.

'I thought he'd brought me on fucking holiday not to be a fucking distraction and to watch his back,' she blurted out emotionally to anyone who would care to listen, although Kay was the only person there to hear.

Kay ignored the remark. 'Let me get you a blouse whilst you clean yourself up,' offered Kay, 'and I'll find a janitor on the way.'

'Christ, what a fucking mess.' Then the young lady calmed down a little and spoke through tears. 'That would be good if you could. Thank you … I'll get it all cleaned for you. Promise.'

The young lady, probably twenty-six or twenty-seven, was taller and broader than Kay and so Kay brought her most loose fitting knitted top and some cleaning wipes. 'There you are,' said Kay on her return, 'you look better already.' And she did – well, a little better. This was not the time to interrogate the distressed young lady. That could come later when Kay's clothes were returned to her. 'Will you be okay if I leave now?'

'Yes. Thank you. What's your name?'

'It's Kay. I'm in 208 on Deck 9.'

'208. Okay. I'm Destiny, Destiny Wheeler ... thank's again.'

'No worries. You take care.'

Destiny's boyfriend was waiting outside. He was handsome in a rugged sort of way, cultured but there was an underlying menace about him. Through a contrived smile there was a threat in his eyes as he demanded in English with a slight Irish brogue: 'She alright, is she?'

'She's okay. Upset, I think,' Kay replied avoiding any sense of confrontation or judgement, adding breezily, 'she was sick so I found her some clothes. She'll be okay.' Then Kay walked away just as the janitor conveniently approached.

Back in their stateroom, they didn't need to discuss their next course of action. Their thoughts and abilities always seemed to be in perfect harmony. 'The photo gallery I think', said Mark with a wink.

They moved along the bewildering rows of photographs, probably close on a thousand. Eventually they found photographs of Destiny with her boyfriend and one of the boyfriend alone. These they selected. Mark gave the photographic assistant their details; paid with the *MyWay* app, the photographs and cardboard frames were placed in an envelope, and they returned to their stateroom.

Chapter Eleven

Tuesday, 16th April 2019.
At sea approaching the coast of Costa Rica.

IT WAS A BEAUTIFUL DAY.   The sea was calm, the air balmy and the sunshine warming.   In the not too far distance could be seen the palm trees on the beaches, waves gently caressing the white sands, and the lush forests on the hillside beyond.   The views were enchanting, but they needed to return to their stateroom in time to call Pippa at 16.45 GMT.   Pippa answered almost immediately Kay's call. 'Another task, just one, I'm afraid.'

'It's okay, this is great, all very intriguing,' she said, as always exuding enthusiasm, 'I'm enjoying this.   Just tell me what is needed.'

'Thank you, Pippa.   I'm sending you two photos of a couple of passengers.   Can you work your facial recognition biometric magic and see what you come up with?   The only additional help I can give you is that he's English with an Irish background somewhere, about 6-2, reasonably well educated.   I should be able to get his name shortly, but not yet.   His girlfriend is also English, Londoner I should think, not as well educated, 5-7, very trim figure by the name of Destiny Wheeler.'

They finished their call well in time for their 11am private viewing offered by Gerald Featherstone. They cleared the coffee table and anything that might hint at their profession, but prepared the coffee station, which could always provide a useful point of distraction.

Mr Featherstone tapped on their door at exactly eleven o'clock.

'Good morning, sir,' said a beaming Mr Featherstone as Mark opened the door. 'I hope my visit is still convenient for you?'

'Of course, and thank you for being so punctual. Would you care for a coffee?'

'No, but thank you,' he replied as he followed Mark into the lounge area. 'Good morning, Mrs Faraday,' he said with a smile and little bow, but his eyes were restless.

'Good morning, Mr Featherstone. We've cleared the table for you. Would you like another chair for your case?' she asked as he positioned a stainless-steel case on the floor next to the table.

'I think this will be fine, ma'am,' he replied as he unlocked the case, removed a black coloured silk cloth which he spread on the table in front of him rather like a magician preparing for his performance on stage. A well-rehearsed routine perhaps but there was nothing cheap about him. Mark and Kay sat down as he placed little jewellery boxes on the table and continued to speak. 'Everyone has favourites, of course. I have two,' he paused for the briefest of moments before adding, 'one of which is the emerald.'

Featherstone was charming and professional in manner, tone and presentation, an excellent ambassador for his trade. 'I have always thought of emeralds as captivating. You said, ma'am, that you would be interested in a necklace and, maybe, earrings too, and that you would be very open to suggestions regarding style.'

'Yes, both I hope. I don't usually wear a necklace and usually only gold studs,' replied Kay. 'We would welcome any suggestions you have, Mr Featherstone.'

'I hope you will excuse me then as I have made some assumptions on your behalf.' He smiled anticipating a verbal response, but there were only nods of agreement. 'Diamonds are diamonds,' he said with a slight, dismissive even, shrug as if stating the obvious. 'Diamonds can be seen everywhere, every day; in certain circumstances they may seem common-place and ordinary.' He paused for effect. 'Emeralds are not. Emeralds are unmistakable, often with an historic and interesting background if not a romantic attachment.' He paused again. Kay and Mark knew this to be a smooth performance, but Featherstone's enthusiasm appeared to be real, and he was engaging. 'Their quality has been acknowledged for more than six-thousand years, even worshipped by the Incas and indeed Aristotle considered that they were capable of bringing comfort to those who wore them.' He smiled, a gentle smile, towards Kay as if to acknowledge the personal importance of the jewels to her and what he was saying before adding: 'I believe that emeralds are Her Majesty's favourite jewels.'

'You say that they are her favourites?'

'Yes, so I am led to understand. Her Majesty has a large collection of tiaras, but it is believed that the emerald Delhi Durbar Tiara is her favourite.'

'And from India?'

'The emeralds very probably have their origins in the sub-continent,' replied Featherstone with a smile, clearly delighted to take the opportunity to speak about his favourite precious stones. 'However, all that is known with any certainty is that the emeralds were obtained by Princess Augusta of Hesse-Kassel in 1818 after buying a raffle ticket of all things in a state-sponsored charity. The princess later married Prince Adolphus, Duke of Cambridge and the emeralds were later incorporated into a tiara by Garrards.'

Kay was equally delighted to hear this romantic tale. 'That's a wonderful story, Mr Featherstone. Thank you,' she said, adding with a certain excitement, 'but I suppose we should see what you have brought along.'

'I am delighted to have shared the tale with you, ma'am,' he said as he selected a number of emeralds and placed them on the table. 'Quality varies, of course. What I am showing you are of the finest quality, pure verdant green hue with fine transparency, their index of refraction certificated, and their quality authenticated.' Featherstone produced some embossed certificates, but these he placed aside as if of little relevance, as if the real and meaningful importance were the stones themselves, their quality and the desire of his clients. Of course, he wanted to gain a good commission, but he was also always genuinely thrilled when the gems he had selected, together with his skill and expertise, resulted in pure satisfaction for his client. 'I will be happy to talk about quality but, if you wish, I have been presumptuous and have attempted to anticipate your wishes.'

Featherstone removed from his case, as if akin to the Holy Grail, a hinged leatherette box containing a silver chain necklace with a beautiful, shimmering green rectangular, eight-sided stone. There was a detached price tag which Featherstone made no attempt to hide, probably realising that Mark would consider the cost to be of little importance. He was right, the cost meant nothing to Mark only Kay's happiness. Kay looked at the pure verdant green hue of the stone set in four delicate gold claws. 'It's beautiful, Mr Featherstone. Not ostentatious, just simply beautiful. A wonderful choice.'

'That is kind of you to say so, ma'am. Some clients favour a surround of silver or diamonds, but that I think can often serve to cheapen and, if I may say, in your case would negate the stone's contrast with your complexion, 'he said with a slight admiring smile.

He was enchanted by her, that was absolutely clear, and could not resist saying something about what he saw as the mysterious beauty of this Oriental woman. It was what was in his mind and his thoughts just tumbled out. 'I believe also that the discreet gold claws add a certain sense of mystery. As you can see, I have taken the liberty to provide a shorter chain, a *princess* of eighteen inches, not an *opera* or *lariat*. The *princess* would, if I may suggest, be a much more flattering length and would mean that the emerald would rest just on or just below your collar bone.'

Mark studied Gerald Featherstone. There was little doubt that he found Kay more than alluring. But it wasn't completely a sexual reaction. Featherstone was like an artist, seemingly delighted to create a small masterpiece. He reverently picked upon the chain and said: 'May I suggest, Mr Faraday, that you might wish to place this around your wife's neck?' Featherstone handed the emerald and chain to Mark.

Kay stood up and walked to the mirror. Mark followed, stood behind his wife and gently fixed the necklace around her delicate neck. She scrutinised the refection in front of her. Kay's smile registered complete approval. 'What do you think, darling?'

But it wasn't what Mark thought that mattered.   He asked: 'You love it, don't you?'

Kay nodded. 'I do. I do.' There was a tinge of emotion as she spoke, 'and it will be a perfect reminder of a perfect holiday.'

Featherstone stood a little to Mark's side, pleased to be part of the happy event.

'Thank you, Mr Featherstone. This will be perfect,' said Mark. 'And you have some earrings I think?'

They resumed their seats and poured over the selection of earrings, some simple studs, others *drops* and *dangles*. Studs were good, *drops* better.

'I have a small selection here,' he said, placing six jewellery boxes in a neat row as if the boxes were on parade. 'If I may suggest again, large emeralds or *loops* would not do at all. I would recommend neat studs, *drops* or *dangles* that would accentuate the neck, and would be perfect with an evening gown, a blazer or even a v-neck.'

Kay selected the *dangles*, each consisting of an eight-sided emerald stud with a one-inch gold chain suspending an emerald identical in size to the stud.

Featherstone produced a round mirror from the underside of the lid of his case, handing it to Kay. She turned her head one way, then another. There was no arrogance just a simple admiration of the perfection of the earrings, smiling as if grateful for her good fortune.

'You're happy?' asked Faraday.

'Absolutely. Completely,' she confirmed beaming with pleasure.

'Shall we settle with you now, Mr Featherstone?'

'If that is convenient for you, Mr Faraday, although you could settle when you are passing by.'

'Now would be fine. I prefer to get these things out of the way.'

'Of course. I can have these gift wrapped, let you have the certification and ... '

'No need to gift wrap, Mr Featherstone,' interrupted eagerly a smiling Kay. 'I will wear them this evening.'

'Then let me leave you with the boxes, ma'am,' he suggested as he placed the two navy blue leather boxes on the table. He produced a card reader from his briefcase for his concession. With the payment made, Featherstone collected up his case, then turned to face Mark and Kay. 'You will be wearing these beautiful emeralds this evening, ma'am. I am so confident that you will be completely enchanted with them that should you not be satisfied, please come and see me and, although disappointed that I have been unable to satisfy your requirements, I will gladly give you a complete refund. Meanwhile, I will prepare detailed Certificates of Authenticity.' He shook hands with Kay and Mark and turned and left the suite.

Kay caught around Mark's neck and kissed him, squealing with delight. 'You do like them?' she asked.

'Of course, and particularly on you.'

'He was very good wasn't he?' remarked Kay.

'Yes, and I have to say it was difficult not to warm to him a little. I noticed that he surveyed our suite when he came in, not too sure why, but he was very charming and besotted by you.' Mark reflected for some moments. 'It's an act of course, part contrived, part a performance that fits with his personality. It's part of who Gerald Featherstone is.' Mark reflected again, but a little longer this time. 'But of necessity an act, a performance, nevertheless. A superbly skilful performance that has been polished and polished. And women would find him attractive wouldn't they?'

'Yes, he's very presentable; he's probably quite good company, something of a raconteur. That said, you are a little uncomfortable with him. That's why you paid him now isn't it?'

'Yes. We both develop a sense for people don't we, you often more so than me. The lawyer, the salesman, the politician, the journalist. Often charming, reasonable, courteous people, but there's usually a dark underside. In fact, isn't it our experience that there is always a dark underside, significant or insignificant, and we are both more comfortable when we are cautious? When he was talking about emeralds or the Incas, he was on safe ground and comfortable, but there was a tinge of anxiety when not speaking himself as if he was waiting for the awkward question.'

Chapter Twelve

Wednesday, 17ʰ April 2019.
Puntarenas, Costa Rica.

DETECTIVE INSPECTOR PIPPA BLANCHARD CALLED their stateroom. Kay answered. 'Hi Pippa. This is a pleasant surprise, much earlier than I thought. Is there a problem?'

'Oh no, far from it,' replied Pippa enthusiastically, 'Gerald Featherstone had made the headlines a few years back and so there was plenty of information around about him. Once I got started, you know me, I was like a dog with a juicy bone.'

'Well done,' she acknowledged, 'and useful?'

'Featherstone has an interesting background that might well be useful,' said Pippa as she began to give Mark and Kay details. 'Featherstone's father owned *Wondrous Wood*, a company consisting of a small factory and three major high street outlets in Bath, Cheltenham and Oxford specialising in bespoke wooden furniture. In reality, Featherstone's mother ran this very successful company but she was killed in a car crash on the M5 when Gerald must have been about ten or eleven. Not the mother's fault, some drunk towing a trailer. It all went wrong. She died, the drunk didn't. Must have been difficult for Gerald. Anyway, the father was a gifted craftsman and designer but certainly not a businessman and the company eventually went bankrupt a couple of years later. The result was that Gerald had to leave his fee-paying independent school and became a waiter in an up-market café in Westbury-on-Trym. The café was rather pleasant with an outside seating area that caught the sun and was very popular, particularly with middle-aged and elderly ladies, who were charmed by Gerald's attention.'

'Seven years ago,' continued Pippa, 'as Gerald was clearing tables outside the café, a robbery of a jeweller's shop took place just across the road from the café. Gerald very bravely intervened during which he was injured by one of the baseball bat-wielding robbers. He became quite a celebrity, pictures in the *Bristol Evening Post* showing him in a BRI hospital bed as well as featuring on the *HTV* news, that sort of thing. I spoke with Martin, Martin Ford at the *Post*. He told me that there was a suggestion at the time that he should have received a Queen's Commendation for Brave Conduct or something like that but Gerald made the mistake of allowing a justifiable self-congratulation to develop into boastfulness which never goes down very well. Instead, in recognition of his gutsy action the Lord Mayor presented him with a citizenship award, a framed illuminated scroll, and the jeweller offered him an apprenticeship. Eventually Gerald adopted a more humble approach and eventually became the jeweller's assistant manager, although, I understand, a certain resentment remained, particularly as the drunk only served three and a half years. A little later, Gerald went on a cruise and was attracted to the idea of managing a jewellery concession on board a ship. Like libraries on board cruise ships, many, if not most of these concessions are owned by US companies which allow their managers to become shareholders in the concession and are allowed a considerable degree of freedom to stamp their own mark, as long as they turn a good profit for both parties of course.'

'Must have been a difficult time for him. He's done well, Pippa. What have you been able to glean about his personal life?' asked Kay.

'By all accounts Gerald Featherstone is very presentable and charming and has a very nice one-bed apartment in the exclusive Clifton Court near the Royal West of England Academy. He drives a 1980s Triumph Stag. He plays badminton at Kingsdown when home and tends to eat out a good deal in Whiteladies Road and in fashionable restaurants dockside. He's single but I understand he has had quite a few girlfriends, but nothing long-term.'

'Why not?' asked Mark pointedly.

'Ah, an interesting question,' replied Pippa. 'I understand he becomes besotted very quickly and this frightens them off.'

'Predatory do you think?' Kay probed.

'No, not at all,' replied Pippa. 'I know Janet Keir who plays badminton at the same club. Janet actually went out with him a couple of times. She says he always acts the perfect gentleman and has sometimes acted as something of a mediator at the club when there's been the usual petty disputes or silly unpleasantries that often occur at clubs but would away back away from any personal confrontation. Not his style apparently.'

'But he didn't back away during the jewellery incident?' continued Kay.

'That's true but I've checked the case file. During that incident a middle-aged lady was pushed to the pavement in the doorway who was about the same age as Gerald's mother would have been and Gerald admits that at that moment he saw "red".'

'You like him?' suggested Kay.

'I didn't say that. I've never met him but he seems a pleasant, inoffensive sort of guy. Otherwise, nothing known,' she said referring to records of police cautions or convictions, 'although the owner of the jewellery shop that was robbed, a guy by the name of Edward Bessell, has been interviewed twice in respect of handling stolen goods, once in 2014 regarding a theft from St. Ermine Court near Newport and again in 2017 regarding thefts from Burton Grange in the Quantocks, but apparently only as a *person of interest*.'

'There must have been suspicions regarding Bessell for him to have been singled out for interview?' questioned Kay.

'Possibly. Possibly not. Bessell's shop did, and still does, deal with really good quality antiques, some of which are unique pieces at impossible prices.'

'I know Burton Grange,' remarked Mark, 'and can recall something about the burglary but I've never heard of St Ermine Court.'

'It's a five-hundred-year-old manor house in pleasant grounds, with a history of war heroes, family disputes and a Russian princess. And, as you know, Burton Grange goes back even further with connections with the Hispanic world, tales of love lost and found, debts and vast fortunes.'

Mark did know but he didn't want to put Pippa off her stride and would never seek to deflate any enthusiastic and diligent officer. 'Were any of the stolen items recovered?' probed Mark.

'No.'

'What about Bessell's lifestyle, anything interesting there?' asked Mark.

'He has an apartment in Zion Hill,' replied Pippa, referring to the very desirable Georgian terrace overlooking the

Clifton Suspension Bridge. 'He's single and his main hobby appears to be golf.'

'And his vehicle?'

'A four-year-old BMW3i.'

'That's very useful background, Pippa. Thank you,' said Kay.

'Ah, one other thing. I think you must have been in Acapulco a few days back?' queried Pippa.

'Yes, we were,' replied Kay.

'It might be nothing but earlier today there was an Interpol one-line reference to your ship and an Italian steward by the name of Fransesco Maresca. He was murdered and his body discovered on the outskirts of Chipancingo by a chicken farmer.'

'Chipancingo?' questioned Kay.

'That's the place, north of Acapulco.'

'Well,' said Mark who then remained silent for a long moment, 'that is interesting, Pippa.'

'Sir?' asked Pippa breaking a long silence.

'It's okay, Pippa. Curious, I was just thinking that was all,' said Mark.

* * *

Deputy Chief of Security Lace, in pristine white uniform, approached Mark and Kay's table as they sat eating scones during *Afternoon Tea* in the *Ascot* restaurant. Mark stood and pulled out a chair for Alivia.

'You look a little harassed?' observed Kay with a smile.

'Oh, I probably do but it's fine,' she said jocularly, 'I've just had a really big argument with one of the machines in the launderette which broke down in the middle of the spin cycle.'

They all smiled. 'Otherwise, a good day?' asked Kay as more tea arrived.
'Oh yes and I won with the machine,' she replied with a huge grin. Mark and Kay relaxed into their chairs but they needed to know how much, if anything, Alivia knew about Fransesco Maresca and where her loyalties might lie.

'Any news of the Italian steward?' asked Mark casually as he poured Alivia some tea.

'No, nothing,' she replied as if the matter of an 'absent without leave' steward was in the distant past and no longer of the greatest importance.

'There *will* be news,' said Mark in a slightly less relaxed tone.

Alivia Lace was about to take her second sip of tea but stopped. She tried to fathom the significance of the remark and Mark's tone. She looked curious, suspicious even. '"There *will* be" you say,' she asked. 'I don't follow?'

Mark and Kay looked around the *Ascot* restaurant. It was crowded but not too crowded, certainly not near where Mark, Kay and Alivia were seated in the alcove partially enclosed by white and gold trellis. Satisfied that they would not be overheard, Kay spoke, giving details in such a way as to apply some shock and to test whether Alivia would be on-side.

'Fransesco has been murdered, Alivia.' Kay paused deliberately and eyed Alivia who appeared genuinely shocked. Not an unreasonable reaction thought Kay as Alivia had probably never been this close to a murder in her life. Kay continued choosing words that emphasising the obscenity of the act of murder. 'Fransesco's body was found in a ditch near a chicken farm by the chicken farmer north of Acapulco, at a grubby little place called Chipancingo,' she said using Fransesco's first name to remind Alivia of him as a person and implying that the officers must have a much fuller knowledge than they really had of the location of Fransesco's undignified grave near a hot and dusty chicken farm.

Miss Lace looked uncertain as to what she should do next. She dabbed her mouth with her napkin and was about to leave the table.

'Don't get up, Alivia,' said Faraday, his tone gentle but full of quiet authority.

Alivia, still clearly shocked began to collect herself and resumed her seat.

'How ... how do you know this?' she challenged these two passengers whom she in reality knew very little. For a moment she wondered whether they were the good guys or the bad. She thought of Fransesco, a smiling and hard-working individual. She seemed about to choke, then cleared her throat. 'As far as I am aware, we ... we ... have not been informed of this?' she said hesitantly but with a very slightly offended edge to her voice.

'*We* have been informed, Alivia,' said Kay looking directly at Miss Lace and paused a little before continuing. 'We have been informed because we are both senior police officers.'

For a moment Alivia's mind was in turmoil with conflicting requirements of her role, then she said, 'I should inform Mr Craddock or the Staff Captain immediately.'

'The time for immediacy has passed, Alivia,' said Mark in a matter-of-fact and slightly cold and dismissive way. 'There is no need for immediacy now. Fransesco is dead,

Alivia, and in a lonely mortuary many miles away from the luxury we are lucky enough to enjoy here,' he continued so as to remind her of Francesco's misfortune and her good fortune. 'For the moment we would ask you to say nothing to anyone.'

When people are confronted with the unexpected, they will, as often as not, seek security in the familiar or formal processes. Alivia's response was formal, indeed a little defensive, her tone challenging. 'Do you mind telling me why I … I should say nothing?' she asked.

'It's very simple, Alivia,' replied Kay, her response not practised yet virtually choregraphed with those of her husband. Kay looked at the Deputy Chief of Security for a silent moment, then continued. 'People implicated in the murder of Fransesco Maresca will without doubt be on this ship and you are in a position to help us here.'

Chapter Thirteen

Thursday, 18th April 2019.
At sea, seventeen nautical miles west of the Azuero Peninsular, the Pacific Ocean.

THEY WERE SEATED IN THE LOUNGE AREA of Mark and Kay's stateroom, not too close to their door leading onto the corridor nor too close to their balcony, but as secure from the casual or deliberate endeavours of eavesdroppers as possible. Mark had made coffee and they had been speaking for some little while.

'The usual routine,' said Alivia Lace, 'as we thought it unlikely that Fransesco would return, would be to clear his locker and his property would go into storage. Our sister ship, *Tranquillity II*, will be following us in ten days and the Personnel Department's thoughts were that Fransesco would probably surface and then be allowed to join *Tranquillity II*. *Tranquillity II* and the port authorities have been informed.'

'And no one had searched his locker before you did so this morning?' asked Mark.

'No.'

'Okay,' said Mark in a tone of disapproval. 'Personnel should have done that I would have thought. Anyway, not to worry, that helps us because you have searched it and here we have all his personal property,' he said gesturing to a brown cardboard box, 'which we can go through carefully. Are you happy with that Alivia?'

'Of course.'

'We will methodically record everything as if we were attending the scene of a crime, examining all his clothing, clothes tags, correspondence, notes stuck on the inside of his locker, his diary, toiletries, letters, in fact everything including what you found in his bed space.'

They checked everything. Except for one curious matter they found nothing out of the ordinary. Fransesco's neat but meagre possessions were as expected. There was nothing absent that should have been present or something present that would have been unusual. However, in Fransesco's diary was a large envelope containing a photograph taken from the ship's newspaper of Queen Elizabeth and a scribbled feint pencilled note in his diary by the edge of the page: '*1951 HM*' and '*very angry*' together with photocopies of black and white photographs of the 1953 coronation that appear to be taken from a book.

'It's strange that he should have the photos of the Queen's coronation,' remarked Alivia reasonably. 'Other than serving on a British registered ship, Fransesco only connection with the UK is that he was born in and his family still live in the Solomon Islands, the Queen being their head of state. Otherwise, he has no English

[97]

girlfriend for example, well as far as I am aware he hasn't, or a souvenir collection of business cards from pubs or restaurants in Southampton, that sort of thing.'

'But he has these paper cuttings,' said Mark leafing through a neat collection of cuttings, 'mainly regarding the Chinese who are seeking close ties with the islanders probably because of its strategic position and natural resources including zinc, nickel, lead and gold. We need to confirm the date of the newspaper article and the date he may have taken a book from the ship's library.'

'Why?' asked Alivia, apparently at a loss to understand why.

'Because these dates and pictures were clearly of significance to Fransesco. If that is the case then they are very likely to be of significance to our enquiries.'

***

Mark and Kay had lunch before speaking with Pippa who was, as always, bright, enthusiastic and positive. It was an enlightening conversation.

'Craddock's father had served in the Merchant Navy and was a drunk,' said Pippa, 'who abused his mother. Andrew Craddock left home when he was seventeen and went south and worked in an open-air fruit and vegetable market in Norfolk. He then joined a private security firm, *SeaSure Security*, before joining the Port of Felixstowe

Police, as you know a non-Home Office force.' Mark and Kay would be aware of these arrangements where such private forces are established by statute as is the case with the local Port of Bristol Police with its members being Special Constables. 'He was with the port's police for six years before joining the cruise line as the Assistant Security Chief. He would have been twenty-nine then. After two years he was promoted to Deputy then three years later to Chief, that was four years ago.'

'He's done quite well,' suggested Mark.

'Yes, although, I understand that the job tends to be dead men's shoes. Male officer ranks tend not to stay that long and go home to their wives and children.'

'Is he married?' asked Mark, keen to have an understanding of his lifestyle.

'He's divorced with two children aged nine and eleven.'

'And where does he live?'

'He lives on Sandbanks Road, Dorset, not Sandbanks itself,' she replied, referring to the most expensive real estate in the country, 'but a nice enough property with a very slight, partial view of Poole Bay. The house was originally a run-down two-bedroom bungalow owned by a very elderly couple in their nineties who died within months of each other. Craddock bought the place which he seems to have steadily extended and, I assumed, renovated over the last six years. According to Land Registry he bought the property for four-eighty. Now it must be worth one point two.'

'And what does he drive?'

'An old Saab convertible.'

'Hum,' pondered Mark, 'but six years ago he could not have guaranteed his promotion and he must be paying his wife some sort of settlement for her and the children I guess.'

'I wouldn't know, sir,' she replied apologetically.

'No, no, it's fine, Pippa. You have painted an interesting picture and we know from his deputy that he's a martinet and as a manager a bit of a bully, although very close to his immediate boss, the Staff Captain, who considers him to be the epitome of the appropriate tough manager. And you've given us a lot to think about. Thank you.'

'There's been a few delays on the facial recognition front but I shall see if I can identify Destiny's boyfriend within the next twenty-four hours, meanwhile, I have two pictures of the murder victim which I will send to your phones in the next ten minutes if that's convenient?'

'That will be perfect.'

***

The photographs were graphic. Francesco Maresca's throat had been cut clumsily, not with a military or butcher's knife but with what appeared to have been a rusty farm implement and the wound seemed to indicate that he had struggled. Pippa was able to tell them that the post-mortem examination of his stomach contents had revealed that he had consumed a large quantity of *pulque*, a drink similar to *tequila* but much more potent, a short while before his death.

Chapter Fourteen

Friday, 19th April 2019.
Panama Canal.

FOR MANY THIS WAS THE MAIN EVENT of the cruise – the eleven-hour day-time transit of the Panama Canal.

The fifty-one mile long Canal had been opened to shipping in 1914 but not officially until 1920, joining the Pacific and Atlantic Oceans by cutting through the Isthmus connecting the land masses of north and south America, weaving a course that utilised the lakes thus, together, avoiding the hazardous Cape Horn and the 'Roaring Forties' and very substantially reducing the sea voyage miles. The idea of a canal was not new being considered as far back as 1534 to facilitate the transportation of gold and silver from Peru to Spain, at that time the most powerful empire, financially and militarily, in the world. Now a new route incorporating parts of the original Canal had been completed in 2016 capable of taking much larger ships, although the *Tranquillity* would take the original more scenic route with its lush rainforest.

Mark and Kay had breakfast on the After Deck seated with Peter and Sarah Hewer-Scott, leaving the port of Balboa and passing under the Bridge of the Americas. Throughout the transit there was a fabulous carnival atmosphere with traditional Panamanian music, essentially the music of Andalusia, interrupted from time to time by a light but fascinating commentary provided by

Colonel David Hemmings, a retired Royal Engineer. Hemmings' contribution could easily have been dry, monotonous and overburdened with facts, but Hemmings was a gifted and knowledgeable speaker who added to the sense of adventure. The choice of a Royal Engineer was a sound one as the Canal had been built between 1906 and 1914 by the US Corp of Engineers under the energetic and imaginative command of General George Goethals.

Hemmings, to the delight of the British passengers was able to inject into his contribution excitement by gleefully pointing out the grinning crocodiles basking on the banks in the sun and with tales of daring-do, of the piratic activities of Sir Francis Drake and the questionable exploits of Sir Henry Morgan as well as those of Captain William Bligh's unsuccessful attempt to round the Horn which set in train the later mutiny on the *Bounty*.

Attractive stalls had been placed around the Sun Deck with displays of local hand-crafted jeweller, wood carvings, ceremonial masks and colourful pottery. BBQ food was in abundance throughout the day including local dishes such as *ceviche*, a seafood dish and *empanada* pastry.

As the *Tranquillity* passed through the Culebra Cut, passengers were entertained to a vibrant display of the *salsa* performed by Edmundo Gardel and Nestor Virta, a performance made even more exciting by the accompaniment of the *tumbadoras*, the conga drums.

Mark and Kay could see Craddock from time to time. The entertainment enjoyed by the passengers was contagious and Craddock was swept along with the carnival atmosphere in a sort of excitable escapism yet, on occasions, he could be seen at the handrail looking out across the lakes deep in anxious thought. He certainly was deep in thought, something not unnoticed by Mark and Kay. His thoughts were of the steward, Fransesco, an innocent, and the retribution that seemed to have befallen this young man. He doubted that it would ever be possible for him to avoid similar retribution if he should fail.

Meanwhile, Kay purchased a *pollera*, a traditional ruffled blouses worn off the shoulders, originally worn by lowly female servants but later adopted by the upper-class.

As they sailed across the tranquil Gatun Lake, Mark and Kay met with Alivia over a lunch time grilled *Moorland* sirloin with *Rock 'n' Soul* music playing in the background. They told Alivia what had been discovered about Craddock, his career and family. As they spoke they were approached by Destiny who thanked Kay for her help in the ladies rest room and checked whether Housekeeping had returned the clothes that Kay had loaned her.

Destiny excused herself and walked towards the bar only to be confronted by her boyfriend. 'What did you say to them?'

'What do you mean?'

'You said something?' he demanded, squeezing her upper arm and pushing her discreetly away from the bar.

'I wanted to check that Housekeeping had returned her clothing, that was all. I don't know what you are getting so worked up about. They're just passengers.'

'You don't speak to them again. Do you understand me?' he said, his facial expression and stance one of ill-concealed aggression and dominance as he tightened his grip.

'Why can't I speak to them?'

'They're cops.'

***

They went to their bed earlier than usual but before they finally fell asleep they had picked up the simple text from Pippa that was sent at 07:00 GMT:

'Robert O'Connor aka David Kennedy CRO'.

Chapter Fifteen

Saturday, 20th April 2019.
Cartagena, Colombia.

HE TAPPED ON THE DOOR OF STATEROOM 208. He waited. The weak link. The person who could potentially provide useful information to Mark and Kay that would otherwise be problematic for them to secure. He wasn't sure of the reason for his invitation. But he waited. Uneasily.

Those inside wanted him to wait for just a few minutes. A few minutes would be long enough to generate a little anxiety – a potentially useful ingredient for the interview of a *person of interest*. He remained standing in the corridor and wasn't sure if he should knock again. But there was no need. Kay Yin opened the door.

'Ah, Mr Pitman.' Her smile was disarming. 'Please step through.' They walked into the lounge area of the stateroom. He eyed Mark Faraday and Alivia Lace. An anxious smile creased his face. His eyes betrayed his unease. 'Would you care for a coffee, Mr Pitman?' asked Kay.

He noted that coffee cups were on the table, already half empty. They had been talking he concluded correctly. 'That would be kind of you,' he replied, his nervous eyes darting about as he noted three ominous buff-coloured files that had been placed before three of the seats occupied by Mark and Alivia, and he assumed Kay. 'White please,' he asked.   A slight nervousness tinged this request.

The coffee cup was placed on the table. Kay beckoned Pitman to the fourth seat, the empty seat, and spoke first. 'I think it best if we tell you where we are at, Mr Pitman,' she said seriously implying that their investigation was on-going and advanced. 'We are police officers. You know that of course because you revealed our identity to Mr O'Connor.'

'I don't know what you mean,' replied a clearly confused and unsettled Pitman, adding hopefully: 'I don't know a Mr O'Connor.'

'Ah, but you do, Mr Pitman,' said Kay slowly with a smile but firmly as she raised her index finger, 'although he's sailing under the name of Mr David Kennedy. And he's a Mason as are you.'   This unnerved Pitman, a flutter of panic gripped his chest as was intended. What more did these officers possibly know he wondered?

'By way of clarification, I am Detective Superintendent Yin and my husband here is Chief Superintendent Faraday.' Kay picked up her buff file, opened it and appeared to carefully refresh her memory by reading some scribbled notes that were in fact complete gibberish. But of course, Pitman didn't know this. After a few moments Kay closed the file thoughtfully and fixed Pitman with her dark penetrating Oriental eyes.

'We also know, Mr Pitman, that you are engaged in smuggling with Craddock.' Pitman's body now became rigid, full of tension, his face creased with an alarm impossible to disguise. He wasn't expecting this and tried without success to formulate in his mind a convincing reply. He was about to respond but was silenced by Kay who raised an index figure again. 'Craddock is the main player, of course. Not you.' She paused giving Pitman a little time to consider the advantageous implications of that remark which provided him with a glimmer of hope. His taught facial expression relaxed - a little. 'Your joint smuggling activities have formed part of the pantomime performance on the quayside with the boxes with the red crosses.'

For Pitman, this revelation was like a visit by the *Grim Reaper* at midnight He became completely still seemingly transfixed by Kay's forensic-like glare. 'This smuggling takes place at each port of call, although not so at Huatulco.' As Pitman listened, the only conclusion he could draw was that these officers must be well informed, although, in reality, their knowledge was virtually non-existent.

Now it was Mark's turn to provide imaginative background to support Pitman's own self-generated conclusions whilst, at the same time, encouraging a response whilst seeking confirmation and information.

'And the flat packed boxes are stored in the Security Locker?' interjected Mark, referring to a secure room about two-thirds the size of a stateroom on Deck 3 with an inner cage containing a large vault.

'Yes.'

'And the keys are held by Craddock and yourself, just two sets, but not a set for Miss Lace here?' asked Faraday, knowing full well that Pitman's answer would be totally implausible.

'I give Alivia a set when necessary,' Pitman replied without offering a convincing explanation. It was a patently ridiculous answer and Pitman knew it to be so, thus adding to his discomfort and unease.

'Hum,' said Mark dismissively. 'Before we move on, I'm intrigued to know,' asked Mark, 'how a man like you from a very respectable background got himself mixed up in all of this. Your father is the highly regarded headmaster of a prestigious independent school. Your mother is a magistrate and at one stage the High Sheriff of the county who, in past years not that long ago, was required to witness executions no less.'

Mark had included, what many might have been considered a flippant and irrelevant remark, but it was made partly to insert an unsettling element of humour, the reference to executions also underlining the significance of the ancient office and his mother's standing in the community. He smiled at Pitman and moved his head gently from side to side as if in critical disbelief.

'Your brother is a first lieutenant in the Royal Navy and here are you in disgrace.' Mark paused so as to allow Pitman to reflect upon this comparison, his vulnerability, his family, the embarrassment of it all.

'Here's the thing, Mr Pitman,' explained Kay firmly. 'Craddock can't help you. He's in what I think one American president once described as "deep, deep do-do". All that will be on his mind when he is arrested will be how to get out of this deep, deep do-do, and to limit his culpability as a smuggler.' Pitman shuddered slightly at the ominous thoughts of arrest. The slightly amusing reference to the American president merely cemented again in his mind the conclusion that the officers were full of confidence.

Kay continued: 'One avenue for Craddock, and I suspect the only one, is to shift the blame onto you.' Pitman began to see the worrying logic here as the two officers allowed him to reflect upon his precarious and uncertain future. A few moments of silence passed, then Kay added: 'The only people that can help you are seated around this table.'

'How did he draw you into this?' asked Faraday providing another unsettling deviation which served to keep Pitman constantly on the back foot, unsure who would ask him the next uncomfortable question.

'I got into debt', he replied without hesitation, as if debt was an innocent and reasonable justification, a situation that most people would find themselves, as he engaged in the mental gymnastics of rationalization and obscuring from his mind that his activities were actually criminal. 'He offered to help. He gave me £1,000. It wasn't enough, the truth be told, but it certainly helped.'

'Then he asked you to do little jobs for him?' continued Kay which Pitman interpreted as Kay being full of understanding for his plight.

'Yes. To liaise with port officials. Take packages ashore. One day he asked me to stand guard over some empty cardboard boxes, the one's with the red crosses. I didn't really think about it, I just did as I was asked, but later in his office he told me that between the leaves of the cardboard boxes were thin layers of cocaine. He laughed and told me not to worry about it.' Mark and Kay's facial expression displayed no surprise at this revelation; however, this was the perfect opportunity for the officers to discredit Craddock, negate the control he had over Pitman and undermine Craddock's authority during this conversation.

'Craddock isn't very clever,' offered Kay dismissively as if disappointed. 'This ploy of concealing drugs between the cardboard leaves of boxes is regularly employed by

Chinese smugglers using the airports at Sydney and Melbourne.'

Whilst Mark and Kay's expressions displayed no surprise at all, Alivia's expression was one of utter shock.

'Are you mad, Bob. Whatever possessed you?' Alivia asked.

'Once you are in, Alivia, you are in,' he replied sharply and defensively as if he was now somehow a duped and vulnerable victim. He was silent for a short moment deep in thought. 'You're never out, Alivia,' he said almost mournfully. 'Craddock reminded me of this when we were in port at Acapulco and there was more news about cartel murders of traitors or even the murder of those they believed might be treacherous. Craddock has given me various sums of money but warned me of the consequences of telling anyone.' He looked at Kay with a resigned expression. 'What else was I supposed to do?'

'Miss Yin told you that we can help you,' said Mark full of reassuring confidence. 'That won't be too difficult for us. The greater difficulty you face will be for you to help yourself.'

Pitman looked perplexed. 'I'm not sure what you mean?'

'It's very simple,' replied Mark. 'From this moment onwards, you will act as if this conversation never took place. In fact, you will not discuss with anyone our conversation here today. You will act as you do every day as you go about your daily duties. You will act as you always do with Craddock and Miss Lace. There will be no whispering in dark corners or furtive glances over your shoulder. If you see Miss Yin and me about the ship you will not avoid us but acknowledge us as you would any passenger normally. If you wish to communicate with us you will do so by pretending to respond to a query from us about the ship's itinerary. To help with that illusion we will always carry with us the ship's daily paper,' then added in a much firmer tone: 'Do we understand each other?

'Yes, yes, I understand.'

'I sincerely hope you do, Mr Pitman. It might be an idea,' suggested Mark, 'that as Craddock might challenge you shortly that you go and sit in one of the cubicles in the public toilets in the corridor for twenty minutes and reflect quietly. Get yourself in the right frame of mind for what the future potentially could hold for you which will either be grim or not so grim.'

Pitman made an almost resentful smirk as if Faraday was mocking him.

'It's a prudent suggestion, Mr Pitman,' interjected Kay. 'The corridors of this ship are covered by CCTV as you know. It may be that Craddock will become aware of your visit to us today. If Craddock asks where you have been, I suggest you tell him that Mr Faraday was concerned that one of his cufflinks is missing, that he is not accusing our steward of theft, but it is missing and he thinks that he lost it in *The Globe* or walking to or from. You can tell him that it is of enormous sentimental value given to Mr Faraday by his father and embossed with the crest of The Fire Service College at Morton-in-Marsh, Gloucestershire. I'm sure that the detail of such an explanation will sound persuadably unusual but, more importantly, authentic. For the moment, you should ensure that your *Report of Missing Property* records are endorsed accordingly should Craddock check.'

'Meanwhile,' probed Mark, 'Craddock is unlikely to deliver the drugs port-side in cardboard boxes. How does he plan to get them off this ship?'

'He's going to use medium-sized buffers, the type we use on the larger lifeboats or used by the pilots and Channel fishing boats.'

'And he's going to decant the cocaine from the plastic envelopes in the lining of the cardboard boxes into these buffers in the Security Locker. That's why Miss Lace isn't given a key?'

'Yes,' he replied, embarrassed as he looked at Alivia now that his disloyalty and dishonesty had been revealed. 'I'm sorry, Alivia.'

'You let me down, Robert, and this ship.'

'Miss Lace is quite right,' said Kay, 'but for the moment, both of you must resist the temptation to engage in recrimination or justification. If you do, someone will overhear you for sure or simply guess. Act as you normally would, difficult as that will be. For you, Mr Pitman, your freedom depends upon it.'

'And the buffers,' continued Mark, 'the insides can be easily accessed?'

'Yes, they are flat packed for ease of storage. There's a removal valve about the size of a 50 pence piece and they can be pumped up.'

'Okay, Mr Pitman, your cooperation is noted and appreciated.' Pitman stood up and was walked to the door by Kay, reassured that his conduct would now be more favourably considered.

'Don't forget the *Missing Property* report,' reminded Kay.

***

Once Pitman had left, Alivia asked: 'How did you know I didn't have the keys for the Security Locker?'

'Because I'm sure that you would have told us if you had,' Kay said. 'We had assumed that you could not have resisted poking about and you would have discovered the flat packs.'

'Oh, right. But what about all the other stuff. How did you know that?'

'We didn't,' replied Kay as she poured more coffee. 'You supplied details of his family and employment history. Your records showed that his hobby was his Triumph Stag sports car, a beautiful and elegant icon of the 1980s but expensive to run and maintain. We build on what we know and so, for example, the question in our minds would be, why that sort of car? The best guess would be to impress, and what we know of his conduct supports that view. Whilst all his meals on board are free, drinks are not and your records show that he is a very generous host with a very expensive bar tab. If he's spending this sort of money when also on shore leave we would suggest that he must be in debt.'

Mark continued the theme as Kay poured Alivia her coffee. 'He was a junior floor manager in The House of d'Arcy, the department store, the nearest the city of Southampton has to Harrods. The company has closed its stores in Manchester and Harrogate and were "rationalising", I think that's the term they use, the Southampton branch and one way they did this was by making redundant their security manager and required Pitman to take on the role of overseeing the contracted security staff as well. It's all in the Personnel file you obtained for us. The company sent him on a three-day internal security managers course, but Pitman could clearly see the writing on the wall and when the job of Assistant Chief of Security on board this ship was advertised, he jumped at it. In many ways he was an attractive candidate. D'Arcy's is a well-known prestigious store, the *Tranquillity* is a well-known prestigious ship and for Pitman the rank insignia of the Assistant Chief of Security is identical to that of his brother's Royal Navy rank. It was a job impossible for him to resist. But one problem remained. The difference between his salary and that of his brother was significant and here in lay the recurring problem for him. Pitman would want to live up to his perceived or proclaimed status and his debts no doubt have not diminished as a consequence.'

'But you couldn't know that for sure?'

'No, we couldn't,' replied Mark. 'You often never do when interviewing. Interviewing a suspect with a string of convictions and known MO is one thing but when you are faced with a new or unknown suspect you are often dealing with a blank canvas and have to delve into the deeper recesses. We do have to make intelligent assumptions. We would also study a suspect's reactions. Consider his responses and body language. We would confront a suspect with compelling logic. We would provide him with attractive options. We manoeuvre his thoughts so that he would be encouraged to answer truthfully. We surmise and join up the dots imaginatively. Very often there are no dots for an investigating officer but you very helpfully supplied us with many of the dots. This is all we did with Pitman.'

'That's brilliant.'

'I'm not sure it was brilliant,' said Kay, 'Mark and I often work together and we've been at this game for some time.'

'We know how each other thinks which is very useful.' Mark and Kay looked at each other and exchanged affectionate smiles before Mark continued. 'We rarely over-talk each other which will inhibit the flow of our thoughts and the flow of the interview. Anyway, can I suggest, Alivia, that you and Kay liaise as you jog around the deck. You are both athletic and Craddock know we are police. It would be quite reasonable that you would both share common interests?'

'I don't think,' said Kay, 'that there is a rush for anything. Craddock isn't going anywhere, unless he's a very strong endurance swimmer that is,' added Kay with a laugh, 'and we have another important job for Pitman to perform for us.'

'You mentioned "body language",' questioned Alivia keen to increase her knowledge and play her part.

'Ah yes,' said Mark, 'always important, very often of critical importance. It's all about gestures, postures, position and distance; the non-verbal aspects and implications of face-to-face encounters, that sort of thing. If we are speaking to someone, body language will tell us a great deal about the person's attitude and confidence, even his thoughts and if he's being untruthful. Even if you are not speaking to someone directly but observing them from a distance, their body language can also tell us a great deal. Of course, you can always arrive at the wrong conclusions. You only have to look around this ship. What the passengers and crew say, or what they do, may be absolutely appropriate. On the other hand, sometimes their behaviour may appear inappropriate, bizarre even or simply in bad taste but could, in fact, be their very reasonable reaction to events.'

'I don't follow?'

'Well,' suggested Kay, 'let's think of an extreme example. Mr Sutton died on board, did he not,' she said referring to a seventy-one year old passenger who had suffered a heart attack a few days before, 'yet that evening Mrs Sutton arrived for dinner wearing one of her finest frocks and then spent much of the evening dancing. Was this a defence mechanism in play, with Mrs Sutton making a jolly good job of having great fun and "manning up" and "putting on a brave face". Was this what the psychologists call *denial*? Was this *dissociation*? Was this *suppression*? Maybe his death was a happy release for her after years of tolerating the oppressive dominance of her husband. I'm not saying for a moment that Mr Sutton was like that, in fact later she may have returned to her suite and collapsed on the bed in tears of deep sadness. I wouldn't know. But, what might appear to be in bad taste or bizarre or unusual, might be a quite reasonable and understandable response.'

'I'm trying to get my head around how, in extreme circumstances, people would see things so differently.'

'Let me test you and give you another example', offered Mark. 'A ninety-three-year-old husband rang the police at about 8.30am to say that his wife had died. I attended the scene. The old gentleman met me at the front door dressed very formally in a smart dark suite which he thought was respectful and appropriate for the occasion. He showed me upstairs to their bedroom. They had single beds. The wife had had cancer and had lost a tremendous amount of weight. Her head was centred on a neatly arranged pillow with her bony hands laid neatly outside the quilt, looking like a corpse from an ancient Egyptian tomb. There was a side table on which was arranged neatly a glass of water and a box of paper tissues. I asked the old gentleman when his wife had died and he answered very precisely: "Nine twenty-three last evening." I asked why he hadn't contacted the police earlier and he replied: "I wanted to spend one last evening with her." I thought it was a loving and reasonable response. They had been married for sixty-nine years.'

Mark and Kay could see that Alivia Lace was wrestling with her thoughts. 'But he could have murdered her,' suggested Alivia.

'Yes, he could well have, but I doubt it very much after looking around the bedroom and speaking with the gentleman, speaking with her doctor and noting the husband's reactions when the undertakers came and his demeanour once his wife had been finally taken away and he was alone. In any event, it certainly wouldn't be in the *public interest* to pursue such an investigation.'

Alivia Lace appeared sceptical.

'Let me think of another example, maybe one that is not so dramatic,' said Mark hoping to satisfy her scepticism. 'I recall a case where I had to ask a fiancée to identity a body. She agreed but, as she was seated waiting to go into the chapel which formed part of the city's mortuary, a ghastly place incidentally, she asked me to comb her hair so that she would "look good for him" which, of course, I did. Some would say that that was a ridiculous thing for her to request but, to her, it was important. Maybe it gave her confidence to cope at this emotional moment and provided an opportunity for her to show respect to the person she loved.'

Mark allowed Alivia to reflect for a few moments, then said: 'These were extreme example I know but little we do is done in isolation and everything we do has the potential to provide us with clues as to our thoughts and the reasons for our behaviour. Anyway, let's return to more cheerful conclusions. 'There's Mr and Mrs Knight,' he said, 'who are plainly protective towards their very attractive, but I suspect wayward, daughter who has attracted the attention of a rather dashing young man on, I think it's Table 12, who dines with his parents. The young man's parents seem to be resigned, if not rather pleased with their son's latest conquest, whilst the young lady's parents are clearly unhappy. I suspect that there will be little chance of preventing the inevitable, and the young lady's parents will probably engage in a combination of denial or rationalisation or elements of *cognitive dissonance* in order to cope with what they believe to be an undesirable association. It's human behaviour, it's what human beings do.'

'And what do you think about Mr Kennedy?' asked Kay of Alivia.

'A nasty piece of work, I would say,' she replied without hesitation. 'He's a charmer but he has an unattractive streak in the way he uses his partner, he dominates her and I don't think she is happy.'

'Isn't she?' questioned Kay provocatively.

'You wouldn't be happy if Mr Faraday treated you that way?' challenged Alivia.

'Ah, but I'm not Miss Wheeler,' replied Kay with a beaming smile.

'Miss Wheeler would probably rationalise her behaviour,' suggested Mark. 'Her partner is handsome. True, Miss Wheeler is physically attractive although not particularly sophisticated, and she must realise that other women find him attractive. That would make her feel good, boost her ego and confidence. He's a charmer and I'm sure he can be attentive to her when he thinks it necessary. She will probably excuse his behaviour when he asks her to understand him and forgive him. At that moment she will be wanted. That's a powerful incentive – everyone needs love and affection, companionship and understanding, even if imperfect. In any case where else is she to go? I doubt whether there would be much sympathy for her predicament if it were known. I suspect most passengers would think, if they gave her any kind thought at all other than rather licentious thoughts, that she is a bit of a trollop on the make.'

'Do you think she's on the make?'

'Maybe,' replied Kay, then reflected. 'Probably a little, although I suspect that she is trapped in a relationship, a relationship that isn't perfect but one that is tolerable and has certain compensations.' Kay poured more coffee for them and spoke as she did so. 'I think Miss Wheeler has been "around the block a few times" and is probably realistic enough to know deep down that her shelf-life is limited, and she will inevitably be replaced by a younger version.' Kay thought for a moment, her inherent kindness showing through. 'On the make? Maybe, whatever that means,' she continued, 'I'm speculating. I don't think she is too bright. I might be wrong, but I don't think that she's a bad person. She just peripheral to what's going on, stage scenery. Let's hope that life if kind to her, although I doubt it will be.'

'And then there is the German couple. They intrigue me,' said Mark. 'They always sit at a table tucked away in the corner, yet most passengers seem to be attracted to the window tables with the delightful evening views as we leave port and steam along the coast or sit with a view of the grand staircase or gallery so that they can see other passengers come and go.'

'You mean the Heckhausens. Where they sit, why does that concern you?' queried Alivia.

Mark looked across towards Kay and raised an eyebrow. Kay took the lead. 'It doesn't concern us as such,' she said, 'we just wonder why.'

'And your conclusion?' asked Alivia, eager to know more.

'Um.' Kay paused, then smiled. 'They are not in the limelight are they. They melt into the shadows, they can see but can't be seen, certainly not clearly,' suggested Kay. 'It might be nothing more than that they are "grey" people comfortable in their private little world, doing exactly what we are doing.' But the reference to 'grey' people was lost on Alivia.

'And then there is Mr Featherstone,' said Mark with a smile, 'who has a girlfriend on board.'

'Has he?' asked Alivia eager to hear of any sort of scandal.

'I would think so,' suggested Mark. 'There's an attractive brunette in one of the cosmetic concessions, a Miss Ash of Calvin Klein I think. Their conduct gives the game away. When they talk they do not do so in their *intimate* or *personal zones*, that would be unprofessional, but in their *social zone* appropriate for their roles on board. But his stance and eye contact does however concentrate purely on her whilst there is a slight hesitancy on her part. His head is always directed towards her whilst her eyes are sometimes slightly down-cast. She is a very attractive young lady, and he is an attractive man and appears confident. A natural enough thing to happen on a beautiful ship wouldn't you say.'

Alivia reflected for a moment as she drank her coffee, then asked: 'Do you think Craddock or Pitman are capable of being involved in a murder?'

'We are all capable of murder if the right combination of circumstances present,' suggested Mark. 'I knew a chap who was the manager of a half-way house which assisted offenders released from prison back into mainstream life. He had a conviction himself. A conviction for manslaughter. He was a decent hard-working chap with no background of violence. But he had come home unexpectedly early one evening from his job as the assistant manager in a local timber yard and found his wife enthusiastically enjoying sex across the kitchen table with the next-door neighbour. Before he could control himself, he picked up a kitchen knife and stabbed the neighbour to death.'

'But Robert Pitman?' queried Alivia.

'More likely Craddock than Pitman,' suggested Kay. 'Pitman is a weak individual. I can't see him belt buckle to belt buckle stabbing someone, watching the terror on his victim's face and the life fading from his victim's eyes, but either of them might be capable of murder, arranging a murder, maybe. Whatever, someone on this ship was involved in the murder of Fransesco Maresca. We are sure of that.'

***

The interview with Pitman had not over run the time that they had anticipated. Mark and Kay had judged it perfectly. Their timing had been good. It was now a little past eleven o'clock as they leaned over the teak handrail and waited. They could see Craddock on the crowded and bustling quayside below. He was waiting too. He kept looking at his watch. He kept looking towards the port's entry gates. Then would check his watch again. As time slowly went by his body language had gradually changed. He became impatient or was it agitated, strutting about as if he was engaged in important and legitimate tasks or simply occupying his time only to relax when a small panel truck with a roof mounted refrigeration unit arrived and parked under his direction. Craddock walked up the ramp and entered the ship, returning to the quayside with Pitman carrying red crossed boxes, only two, and took them to the panel truck. Once loaded through a sliding side door, they were exchanged for seven red crossed flat packs. Papers were exchanged and now, no one seemed to be in a hurry at all. Craddock appeared relieved and he and Pitman casually chatted to the truck driver, jokes seemed to be made and all appeared to be light-hearted and above board.

A performance thought Mark as Kay used her *Brunton BAK4* pocket monocular scope to identify the logo on the side of the truck. 'If I've translated it correctly,' she said, 'the truck belongs to "The Holy Church of the Immaculate Redemption"'.

They smiled at each other then began to laugh, rather loudly, at the audacity of it. Mark commented: 'Maybe Craddock is hedging his bets. Maybe he hopes that the connection with the Almighty and the church might be useful when he seeks redemption later on.' Kay put her arm around Mark's waist and hugged him as he put a hand along her shoulder and kissed her on the head, distracted for a moment by the scent of *Five Forty*.

After a short while Craddock shook hands with what appeared to be a very grateful truck driver who then climbed into the cab and drove towards the exit gates. Mark and Kay exchanged glances. For all practical purposes it didn't make sense. The next port of call was Aruba, just 115 nautical miles further along the coast and one day's sailing away. Not enough time for *Tranquillity* to accumulate seven boxes of 'best before' food products for the poor, unless the needs of the poor of Aruba were greater than those of Colombia. But, of course, it did make sense. Complete sense. Colombia is rated as the world's largest producer of cocaine, although the country had since 2000 reduced its illicit production by sixty per cent and drug related violence by fifty per cent. That said, the illicit contents of seven boxes would certainly offset some of the losses in the English Channel.

There was nothing to be gained by Mark and Kay peering any longer. Lunch beckoned and their excursion to Castillo San Felipe de Barajas was scheduled to depart at 2.30pm.

***

Cartagena was a delightful and vibrant city of Baroque colonial streets and squares; houses painted yellow, light blue, dark blue and green, with flowers cascading from wrought iron balconies; classical Spanish-styled churches; and pavement cafes under inviting white- or yellow-coloured parasols were to be found in every street providing much needed shade for their patrons. The castle of San Felipe itself dominated the city as it had done since 1536, protecting the port and its sixteenth and seventeenth century shipments of silver from Peru and destined for Spain. It was massive with nearly seven miles of curtain walls and, remarkably, had only been taken by siege or direct assault once, and that was in 1697. Since that date the fortifications had been improved with a complex system of bunkers, parapets and tunnels that proved impregnable to attacks by pirates, the French and the English and useful for today's illicit drug trade.

The sun was high in a cloudless sky. The heat was intense and tiring and visitors stopped regularly to drink bottled water. It was a steep climb to the battlements up a sloping causeway, but once the summit had been reached, 135 feet above sea level, the commanding and panoramic views were well worth the exertion – and reception was perfect as they received a text from Detective Inspector Pippa Blanchard: *'Update from Interpol: Luis Cabrera arrested for murder of steward.'*

'Thank you,' typed Kay. *'Wait one.'* Mark began to scroll through his phone.
Here it is,' he said to Kay as he handed her his phone containing the details.

'Mark knows a contact down there, they were students together at Quantico,' she typed, referring to the FBI Academy. *'I'm sending you the details now.'*
Kay forwarded the detail. *'Commissary Andrés Nájera, Policia Federal Ministerial. He is the equivalent of a Superintendent with the force's International Directorate.'*

'Okay, will do.' There was a pause as Mark spoke in Kay's ear.

Kay typed again.

'Thank you, Pippa. Oh, and Mark says: "Ask if Cabrera took out any insurance".'

'No worries. Can do.'

***

They dined that evening in *The Silverstone* restaurant. Mark chose the *Grilled Mahi Mahi Steak* with chopped capers black olives, tomatoes and anchovies. Kay, the *Braised Lamb Shank with Colcannon potato* and red wine sauce. After dinner, which included ice cream, of course - *Vanilla Honeycomb Surprise and Oriental Ginger* - they strolled through the ship and made their way to the Photo and Video Gallery.

There were no portraits or posed photographs of the Heckhausens, unusual for passengers, but they found four showing them returning to the ship from excursions with other passengers. Two were excellent. These they purchased. These images they would send to Pippa. As they made their way to the *Miame Atrium*, they made a point of acknowledging Mr Featherstone as acquaintances would, then relaxed in the *Atrium* and enjoyed listening to *The Tranquillity Trio* consisting of a pianist, Melissa, and two violinist, Lilliane and Eva, playing a selection of themes from well-known films, including the '*Love Theme*' from *Romeo and Juliet*, '*Tara's Theme*' from *Gone with the Wind* and '*My Heart Will Go On*' from *Titanic*. It was a perfect ending to a wonderful day.

Chapter Sixteen

Sunday, 21st April 2019.
The island of Aruba, the Caribbean Sea.

THEY GATHERED AGAIN IN STATEROOM 208. After breakfast. In the stateroom's lounge. Discreet. Private.

'I've checked and double checked,' said Alivia Lace, 'the disembarkation and
boarding records as well as the CCTV for the 14th April and can confirm that Fransesco Maresca left the ship at 14:11 and did not return on board, nor did it appear that he lingered port-side after that time.'

'Can you put the CCTV footage of the ship up on the screen again of Fransesco getting off the ship, Alivia,' asked Mark.

'Yep,' replied the Deputy Chief of Security as her fingers glided easily over the keys of the laptop. 'Here we are.'

The clarity of the images of Fransesco, the other passengers and the dockside were excellent but although the ship's cameras did cover the excursion coaches, they did not cover the entrance gates to the dock. 'Tell me, Alivia, what do you think if you compare Fransesco and the other passengers,' posed Mark, 'What do we see?'

Alivia replied: 'His gait is, what shall I say, eager. All the other afternoon excursion passengers are just sauntering or fussing about. But Fransesco seems to be in a hurry to go somewhere.'

'There you are. It's all about body language and I think you are absolutely right,' agreed Kay. 'He had a job to do and he's off to do it.'

'Yes,' said Mark, 'he's walking with purpose as if he has a task to complete. He's not keeping together with other crew members on a half day outing as would be the usual practice and you tell us, Alivia, that he hadn't booked an excursion.'

'That's true.'

'And Craddock and Pitman?'

Her finger pointed to the screen. 'There's Craddock acknowledging Fransesco on the quayside in quite a friendly way as the steward leaves the ship. In fact they are having a short conversation with Craddock putting his hand on Fransesco's shoulder – an unusually friendly gesture for Craddock I would have thought,' observed Alivia Lace. 'Whatever, we know that Craddock and Pitman did not leave the dock at all that day.' She tapped the cursor and moved about the screen. 'And there is Craddock chatting to the German couple, who incidentally are not German nationals but Latvians.'

'Latvians you say,' acknowledged Kay, 'and quite a lengthy chat. Do you have any idea what they were talking about?'

'Not precisely although Craddock says that they have been at pains to tell him that they are both dentists from Rezekue in Latvia and like the British ship very much. He finds them annoying. Apparently, every time they meet they tell Craddock where they are going or what a splendid day they have had.' Kay and Mark just listened without betraying their thoughts but asked themselves, was this the Heckhausens establishing their credentials?

'Also,' Alivia continued, 'Pitman has done a good job for us. He's photographed Craddock's personal desk diary for the 9th through to the 14th April on his mobile phone and there are no references to Fransesco being required to go ashore, in fact there's no reference to him at all.'

'I just cannot believe that Fransesco goes ashore and is murdered as if by chance,' speculated Mark.

'He could have been mugged,' suggested Alivia.

'Oh yes, that's always a very real possibility, Alivia, he could have been, but mugged for what?' questioned Kay. She pointed at the frozen screen. 'He appears to be carrying nothing with him other than his bum bag. Muggers tend to work in tight groups and target their victims. In this case their opportunities were going to be limited simply because of the relatively short duration that *Tranquillity* was in port. I doubt that muggers would waste that opportunity. And so, a lowly paid steward is unlikely to be at the top of their hit list.'

Mark agreed. 'The reports say that the police could not find his watch, cash or wallet. But this can't be the reason for his death. These missing items wouldn't count as rich pickings, and certainly not sufficient for any mugger to waste time and take the risk of transporting him, dead or alive, to Chipancingo. Therein lies the real question, why was the body discovered in Chipancingo?

'And?' queried Alivia with a smile, 'you have an answer?'

'There can only be one plausible explanation,' suggested Kay, 'and that is whoever killed or arranged for Fransesco to be murdered did not want his body to be discovered until *Tranquillity* had set sail and was way outside Mexican territorial waters and jurisdiction.'

Chapter Seventeen

Monday, 22nd and Tuesday, 23rd April 2019.
The Dutch Antilles, the Caribbean Sea.

THEY HAD SAILED AND ENJOYED ENDLESS SEA VIEWS from their balcony, escorted by swooping and cawing sea birds and the playful pods of dolphins, visiting the islands of Curaçao and Aruba, part of what is often referred to as 'The Dutch Islands' or The Dutch Antilles. Both islands lie only a short distance north of Venezuela but are quite different. Curaçao, the larger of the two, has almost year-long, delightful weather with an average temperature of 27℃ deliciously cooled by the on-shore Trade Winds. The buildings of the capital reflect their Dutch heritage with gabled houses painted with wild pastel shades of colour.

There was no urgency about the island. It was all unhurried and relaxed. They
explored leisurely then Mark and Kay took their morning coffee on the Handelskade alongside the Queen Emma Bridge which consisted of sixteen pontoons stretching lazily across the river, one end of which was hinged at the opposite quayside and opened and closed regularly by way of a twin diesel-driven pontoon at the other so as to allow freighters through. It was strangely restful watching quite large ships pass by, at very low speeds of course, as they made their way further up the river to the inland port.

'Do you mind if I join you?' said the Margaret Rutherford look-alike, interrupting their daydreaming thoughts.

'Of course not,' said Mark as he stood and arranged a chair for their fellow passenger. 'Would you like me to order you a drink?'

'That's very kind. I certainly won't say no,' she replied as she manoeuvred herself comfortably into her chair.

'Tea, a coffee, maybe, or a cold drink?' asked Mark.

'A nice pot of English Breakfast Tea would be perfect. Thank you,' she said as she now adjusted her straw hat which allowed even more grey wavy hair to collapse over her left ear.

Mark ordered two teas and a latte and introduced themselves as they waited for their drinks to arrive. 'Margaret Rutherford,' a 77-year-old lady had a mischievous smile and inquisitive eye. She gave her name as Sybil Bodkin from the city of Exeter, a widow and a retired university lecturer.

'I suspect you were much more than a lecturer, Sybil?' queried Kay.

'Well, I was actually a professor of criminal psychology, but I retired a few years ago,' she replied modestly.

'But an interesting life?' Kay probed.

'It was, and fulfilling,' then she seemed to reflect for some moments. 'My late husband and I were not blessed with children and so we would cruise a good deal which gave me the opportunity to indulge in my hobby of people-watching,' she said leaning forward as she spoke as if such an activity was somehow naughty, then she became a little more serious. 'I suppose I looked upon all my students as my family. I probably shouldn't have done so but I did. I was rather protective of my students. Contrary to what many think nowadays I believe it's much more difficult for students. Academic standards are much higher, employment prospects are often quite limited and competitiveness much greater. But it was a rewarding and worthwhile career, and I worked with some marvellous and gifted people. I also had the opportunity,' she paused and gave Mark and Kay an amused look, knowing that what she was about to say would engender interest and speculation, 'to assist the police with their enquiries as they say.' She smiled as if naughtiness had returned. 'I think you might be aware of what I might mean?'

'Would we, Sybil, I can't imagine why?' queried Mark with a knowing smile as they sipped their drinks.

'I think you may, Mark. I might be wrong, but you are either an army officer or a policeman.'

'My goodness,' said Mark with mock astonishment. 'And why would you say such a thing?'

'Firstly, your grooming even when casually dressed. You bring a new meaning to the phrase "smart casual". You dress carefully, all is co-ordinated and your shoes are beautifully cared for.'

'I think that must be down to Brook Taverner', suggested Mark referring to the superb Yorkshire tailors founded in 1912 who always seemed to offer a perfect range of clothes beautifully tailored.

'Ah, yes, an impeccable very British company. But then there is the way you carry yourself. There is a natural authority about you, no pomposity although, maybe, a slight aloofness. You are supremely assured in the presence of others, although you seem to choose these encounters carefully. There may of course be a reason for that.' Mark's expression remained passive and he did not respond to the observation, not openly anyway although his facial expressions would have undoubtedly done so. 'You appear relaxed, yet you are not slothful; you are alert to your surroundings and those about you.'

'Those are interesting observation, Sybil, and you are quite right. I am a policeman.'

'I read a good deal, but as I say my greatest hobby is to people watch. Everyone is interesting, even the lowly road sweeper or janitor. They all have a story to tell and so I love talking with people too.'

'And what about Kay?'

Sybil turned and faced Kay as she answered. 'Ah, that is a little more difficult because you are so elegant and beautiful, my dear, which can serve to interfere with any objective assessment. You are modest about your captivating beauty, you appear at pains not to flaunt it and there is no arrogance. You have a confidence, a confidence which is not based purely upon your beauty, although you must realise the effect you have upon men. You are like a ballerina. Even when shopping in Waitrose or Ikea a ballerina will walk as ballerinas do. It's all about their many years of training and their discipline. They never lose it. Your walk is full of confidence too which I would liken to a military slow march but at a normal pace, precise, ordered and synchronised,' she paused for a slight moment, then added, 'if that makes any sense at all. The confidence will be based upon your background, your experience of the world, of course, its people and a realistic assessment of your own abilities which, I suspect, have been tested from time to time. You have both been tested and as a result you are both protective of each other.'

Sybil paused for a few minutes as another ship passed by casting a cooling shadow over those seated in the restaurant. 'I have a nephew who serves in the army, the Buffs,' said Sybil referring to the Kent regiment whose name derives from the colour of the traditional facings on their uniform, 'and so I could imagine you passing out at

Sandhurst, Kay, proudly marching with a sword in your hand. Is that near the mark?'

'I did pass out with a sword in my hand, Sybil, but it was at the Royal Hong Kong Police College, after officer training.'

'In better days?'

'Yes, in very much better days, I have to say.'

'And now you serve with the British police?'

'Yes, with Mark, but you said that you assisted the police?'

'It has been such a privilege, with the Devon and Cornwall police, profiling, that sort of thing.'

'There must have been many interesting and demanding cases?' suggested Kay.

'Yes, quite a few. I suppose, however, that the most demanding part was to be constantly objective, rather as a doctor needs to be if performing a post-mortem, to keep a perspective and then to remember later that the good outnumber the bad and, for all its horrors, the world is still a beautiful place. Would you not agree?' she probed.

'The world is a beautiful place,' replied Mark, 'although we have to be constantly alert to the unattractive side of human nature.'

'That's very true,' confirmed Sybil Bodkin, 'All of us, indeed even in our often mundane daily lives, are in so many ways prisoners of our own background, backgrounds that indelibly chart our life's journey.' Sybil neatly positioned her cup and saucer on the table and rose from her chair. 'My apologies, I'm becoming far too serious and beginning to lecture. To be a bore is unforgivable. I think I will wander around over there in Wilhelmina Square and look for some postcards for that nephew of mine.'

'We have been happy to be your attentive students,' Kay said warmly. 'We have enjoyed taking with you.'

'If I may say, I find you a very interesting couple. I would love to chat again,
but could I ask you to keep our conversation between ourselves, I just could not cope with being badgered by passengers who want to know all the ghastly details of some of the cases in which I have been involved.'

'Professor, your secret is safe with us.'

***

Aruba had been very different. There was little dock side activity although fresh fruit and vegetables were taken on board. The island had magnificent sandy sweeping beaches and crystal-clear water, a paradise for snorkelling, which Mark and Kay engaged in enthusiastically, although they seemed more interested in each other than the art of snorkelling. Whilst there was little to see in the capital, Oranjestad, the restaurants offered a remarkable selection of Dutch and local foods including: *Stoba Dicabrito, Rijsttafel Keshi, Pastechi, Ayacas* and *Erwtensoep*.

Whilst fruit and vegetables were taken on board and used to enhance the ship's imaginative menus and provide a local dimension, there was no sign of the red crossed boxes or Craddock shore-side, although whilst docked in Aruba, Pitman did oversee the early arrival and unloading of two large white boxes, which Mark and Kay estimated to be about 36" by 24" endorsed on the sides: 'Aruba Chandlers – Suppliers of Scuba Diving Equipment' and, significantly, signed for them. The island's population would hardly need soup kitchens or the services of The Salvation Army and logistically dealing with the white boxes would create an unnecessary hindrance to cartels, yet the white boxes must have been sufficiently important for Pitman to have taken a personal interest. And they were. The boxes contained inflatable buffers. They would not be inflated by air. They would be inflated with cocaine.

As they sailed from Aruba, they dined with Peter and Sarah Hewer-Scott again. Whilst both were successful business people, the magical cruise encouraged them sometimes to act like newlywed teenagers – not a bad thing thought Mark and Kay - throwing inhibitions to the wind. Dining with Peter and Sarah was a really enjoyable affair. Their meetings were relaxed. They spoke of the counties of Somerset and Lincolnshire; they spoke of the merits of vehicles, Mark favouring the Volvo XC90, its robustness and comfort, whilst Peter favoured the Maserati Levante with its Italian style. There was plenty of laughter and giggles. There was no point-scoring or edge to their conversations. They talked of holiday destinations, a recent visit to London and a weekend break at *The Nare* hotel on the south Cornish coast. During the meal they admired Kay's fine emerald necklace, although whilst Peter and Sarah were keen to purchase mementoes of their holiday, both favoured wrist watches.

After dinner, Mark and Kay, Peter and Sarah, visited Gerald Featherstone's concession which also displayed a splendid range of watches including the Omega *De Ville* and Longines *La Dolce Vita* and the Tissot *Bellissima*. Mark and Kay introduced Gerald then excused themselves, allowing their new friends the privacy of choosing what would almost inevitably be an expensive gift.

'He can't take his eyes off you,' Mark said referring to Featherstone.

'Shush,' replied Kay.

'Ah, but you see, it's a fixation, a fixation that could become intense,' he continued, but only partly with humour, as they walked away, eventually re-joining a delighted Peter and Sarah in *The Globe*.

The Hewer-Scotts had chosen matching TAG Heuer watches. 'We are so glad you introduced us to Gerald,' said Sarah, 'such a helpful man. I also asked him if he could fix my opal ring for me, and he is going to sort it out at our next port of call.'

'That is good. What was the problem, the claws?' enquired Kay.

'No, my fingers have got a little slimmer, well skinny really,' said Sarah wiggling her fingers up and down. 'The stone is quite large and has a tendency to slip off. It was a birthday present from Peter,' she said squeezing his hand, 'and I would be suicidal if I lost it and so the band needs altering. Gerald offered to provide a clip, but I didn't like that too much. It looked rather clumsy, and I would probably lose that too and so I preferred to have a small piece cut out. Gerald says that he couldn't do that on board, but he says he has connections in every port and he will have a small piece cut out for me when we reach Jamaica and have it ready for me before we set sail that same evening,' she said delightfully as she squeezed her husband's hand again.

Mark and Kay made no comment nor did their facial expressions change, but they were thinking exactly the same thoughts. Mark nodded to a waiter as Kay admired Sarah's watch. They relaxed in the comfortable chairs of *The Globe*, but Mark's dyslexic mind was akin to a kaleidoscope of thoughts. He had become distracted by thoughts of the murder of Fransesco, the Nelson alcove and Craddock's drug smuggling, Featherstone's offer to have Sarah's ring altered as well as Featherston's displays of jewellery one of which featured a silver *Manhattan* necklace with matching *drop* earrings. Once they had returned to their stateroom they both wondered if Francesco Maresca had been asked to take some jewellery ashore at Acapulco.

***

They had only returned to their stateroom minutes before when Kay's mobile phone bleeped with an incoming text from Pippa:

"Heckhausen is Oleg Sukhovetsky FSB.
Further confirmation to follow."

Mark and Kay's suspicions had been spot on that the Heckhausens were 'grey people'.

Chapter Eighteen

Wednesday, 24ᵗʰ April 2019.
The Island of Jamaica, the Caribbean Sea.

THERE WAS A CARNIVAL ATMOSPHERE everywhere they went, the constant sounds of rhythmic drum music all around them yet none of it seemed to conflict but naturally merged one with the other. So too the aroma of local cooking, the scent of flowers and spices, nutmeg, cinnamon, turmeric, bay leaves and peppers, the sweet smells of apricots and peaches, and an almost overwhelming opportunity to buy colourful gifts.

As they explored the teeming markets, they saw Mr and Mrs Heckhausen who were completely engrossed with a stall holder who appeared to be explaining how a mechanical children's toy worked. The Heckhausens examined one toy, a drummer, then another, a trumpeter, and yet another which had a silly face and mechanically shuffled its feet forward across a table. Some of these toys seemed to have clockwork mechanism whilst others were battery or electrically operated. And some, not all, played musical tunes. After much deliberation and experimentation with some of the toys falling from the table onto the grass, the delighted Heckhausens chose a 'jack in the box', which played no musical tunes at all, before walking on to stalls that sold everything from kitchen towels to leather belts, shorts and t-shirts, vanity cases and watch straps and a mouthwatering array of fresh fruits. The Heckhausens then spent quite a time at a musical instrument stall where they eventually purchased, after much noisy practice, a set of beautifully painted maracas depicting colourful scenes of the island. There was also the opportunity for Mark to have hair braids. He declined!

***

Mark and Kay ate a barbeque lunch on the After Deck before their tour to Oracabessa Bay and the *GoldenEye* Hotel.

'GoldenEye', the common name of the sea duck, *Bucephala Clangula*, aggressive and territorial, with its distinctive yellow eyes, but also a name that was evocative.

'GoldenEye', a home where author Ian Fleming lived and James Bond was born, where the creator of *'007'* wrote his first spy novel, *'Casino Royale'*, and all his subsequent novels. Not a hotel in the traditional sense but it has two restaurants, a spa, and an infinity pool, a wonderful collection of beautiful and sumptuous beach villas and lagoon cottages, each surrounded by lush private gardens, large verandas and outdoor showers, with stunning views of the idyllic crystal-clear waters of the Caribbean. For most The *GoldenEye* Hotel was the nearest thing to paradise on Earth.

And a visit to the *Bamboo Bar* on Button Beach was a 'must do' for the passengers of the *Tranquillity* and to sip pre-dinner cocktails – shaken not stirred - whilst immersing themselves in myth and tales of murder and mayhem.

***

After dinner of *Singapore Mixed Fish Grill* for Kay and *Paupiette of Beef* and the obligatory ice-cream with *Chocolate Fondant and Mandril Gel* for Mark, they went to the theatre for the evening's second performance of *Phantom of the Opera*, the lead role being taken by Michael Levesque. The show was atmospheric and simply spellbinding, with Levesque dramatically appearing through smoke, with electrifying gestures, domineering eyes starring menacingly at the audience, swirling his long black cape, accompanied by drum beats and the striking cords of violins and then, to the unexpected astonishment of all, the spectacular crash of a chandelier upon the stage. At the end, the whole performance was greeted by a standing ovation.

After the show most of the passengers gathered in the *Miame Atrium*. There was an excited buzz as the performance was discussed and applauded, champagne flowed and glasses clinked. Mark and Kay mingled then saw the Heckhausens deep in conversation with fellow passengers. 'Mrs Heckhausen' drank slowly. Kay waited patiently. 'Mrs Heckhausen' eventually put her empty glass down on to a side table. Kay eventually picked it up.

It was a spontaneous 'long shot', of course, in which Kay had hoped to have been able to secure her fingerprints and confirm her identity by possibly using *nihydrin* from the Medical Centre or silver nitrate from Housekeeping but her later attempts were not those of a fingerprint laboratory and she was not to be successful.

Chapter Nineteen

Thursday, 25th, Friday, 26th and Saturday, 27th April 2019.
The Windward Passage, Greater Antilles, the Caribbean Sea.

THEY STEAMED THROUGH THE WINDWARD PASSAGE between Cuba and Hispaniola, three full days at sea. There was a pleasant sense of relief. Of course, Mark and Kay's minds were still preoccupied with the death of Fransesco Maresca, the drug smuggling, Craddock, Robert O'Connor aka David Kennedy and now the Heckhausens. But at least they were able to relax a little. Craddock, the Heckhausens and Kennedy weren't going anywhere soon and it gave them time to re-evaluate, to distance themselves so to speak and clear their heads, with no early breakfasts, rushing about to disembark for excursions and no pressure at ports. In any event, there was plenty to do to aid their escapism. *The Spa of Tranquillity* beckoned. There were afternoon films choices including *'Operation Mincement'*, *'Murder on the Orient Express'*, *'Mamma Mia'*, *'The Cruel Sea'* and *'That Hamilton Woman'* the 1941 film starring Laurence Olivier in the role of Admiral Nelson and Vivien Leigh as Lady Emma Hamilton. Mark and Kay both played water polo and completed in the table tennis tournaments – with some success. They came third.

In the theatre there was the ship's version of the 'Mastermind' competition and, also in the theatre was staged the ship's excellent production of 'The Antiques Roadshow' hosted by the TV personality, Anthony Beckingsale, aided by Debby de Lange with four of Alivia's security staff present. A very prudent measure with the presence of the security staff adding a little excitement.

'The Antique Roadshow' stage had been set against a backdrop of three large posters to the left, one a 1936 Holland-American Line shipping poster at £4,000, a 1935 New York Central Lines poster of the Rockefeller Centre at between £9,000 and £12,000 and a 1935 Imperial Airways calendar poster by Tom Purvis at £1,600. Two of the security detail remained 'on stage' either side of Anthony as Debby would exit to reappear escorted by two other security officer and an item, the crystal-clear image of which was projected upon a screen to the right. There were twenty-one items displayed during the 'roadshow', the first of which was a filigree-worked platinum ring with a large cut diamond with contrasting calibre-cut blue sapphire accents, from the early 1920s and valued at £16,000. This was followed by a much more modest sterling silver necklace, dated 1932, with faux pearls and emerald green square glass stones of graduated sizes and valued at £400. Numerous other items of jewellery were exhibited, and their significance and provenance explained. The show flowed easily as Anthony gently teased his audience, commenting at one stage about their possible ownership of high-end cars as Debby appeared with a large Bentley 'B' car mascot with two wings at £700.

Knowing the islands that *Tranquillity* had visited, Anthony spoke of wooden carved masks produced by islanders whilst projecting images of two wall masks, one in terracotta by Goldscheider of a young lady with a serine expression and valued at between £400 and £600, and another ceramic profile mask by Cope of Staffordshire at £300. A chair, which most of the audience had probably considered to be a stage prop, was in fact an early 1930s birch wood and padded black leather upholstery 'club' chair by Danish designer Kaare Klinte as well as a Belgian hat stand. Needless to say, Anthony was able to suggest, knowing that *'Murder on the Orient Express'* had been screened the previous day, that Hercule Poirot would have hung his hat on such a stand in the hallway of his London apartment, along with those of Captain Hastings and Chief Inspector Japp, if the latter ever took his hat off, an observation that was greeted with some mild clapping.

Anthony Beckingsale was inundated with questions and requests for his book: *'Antiques for All'*, the pile of which had to be replenished twice. Kay and Mark joined the queue to purchase Anthony's book and asked him to sign it too.

That evening Mark and Kay noticed that Gerald Featherstone sat next to Anthony Beckingsale during dinner at Captain Dunbar's table. The conversation at that table appeared casual enough with Featherstone apparently more interested in eating than talking but, as the evening progressed, Featherstone's demeanour altered to one of evaluation, then engagement with Beckingsale more enthusiastically. Maybe that was to be expected between two men with similar professional interests – but was it wondered Mark and Kay. They had noticed the body language. Certainly, the conversation did not go unnoticed by Professor Bodkin who was dining at the same table.

The following morning on the Sun Deck there was a talk on gardening á la Monty Don. There was also a programme of self-defence techniques given by the handsome and powerfully built Shane Woods, a retired PTI from the Special Air Service, demonstrations that appeared to be very popular with some of the ladies who seemed to require additional coaching from Mr Woods in respect of close-contact techniques. Mr Woods, thought Mark, was just the sort of person you might want 'on side'.
During coffee in the *Venetian Bar*, Mark and Kay were joined by Professor Bodkin. 'Did you enjoy your dinner at the captain's table, Sybil?' asked Mark.

'Oh yes, I had the very delightful *Roast Pork Loin with Baked Apple*, cooked to absolute perfection, and followed by *Gooseberry Cheesecake with Ginger Crumb and Grenadine Sauce,* all very English,' adding, whilst clapping her hands together silently, 'superb.'

'And was the conversation between Mr Beckingsale and Mr Featherstone a delight too?' probed Mark.

'You would have noticed, of course,' she replied with a smile. 'It was certainly interesting. After the main course, Featherstone talked with Beckingsale much more than he had hitherto, mainly discussing the silver necklace with the green glass stones,' admitting, 'which I had assumed to be gems, not glass.'

'But a little later, over coffee I think,' said Kay, 'Featherstone engaged with Beckingsale much more closely, was that your take?'

'Yes, that was so,' agreed Sybil. 'The atmosphere changed a little when Featherstone seemed to take an interest in the security of Beckingsale's items and, particularly, how these were taken on and off the ship. Unfortunately for Featherstone, he didn't read Beckingsale's gestures, did he?' she said with a huge grin. 'His enthusiasm for an answer was linked to him leaning forward and encroaching upon Beckingsale's *intimate space* to the extent that Beckingsale closed him down and spent the remainder of the meal talking to the captain about the ship's propulsion, which was all quite interesting but certainly not the exciting conclusion to the evening I had hoped for.'

They all laughter in unison and nodded in amused acknowledgment. 'Very perceptive.' Sybil Bodkin returned the smiles. 'I know, I know,' continued Mark, 'women are generally much more perceptive than men and seemed to have an innate ability to pick up non-verbal signals and possess an accurate eye for detail.' He looked towards Kay full of admiration. 'And thank goodness they do.'

Chapter Twenty

Sunday, 28th April, 2021.
The island of Saint Lucia, the Caribbean Sea.

THEY MET IN STATEROOM 208 with Alivia Lace, a regular occurrence to exchange views. Today their main focus was to be Fransesco Maresca and his diary notations.

These meetings tended to be very relaxed but, nevertheless, serious and followed an unwritten agenda. But today the meeting would certainly be less relaxed, more serious, the only agenda item being Fransesco's notebook entries.

'I think we should explain fully what we believe is a crucial development. The truth is I have fouled up,' said Mark. 'I keep returning to these entries, the majority of which are neatly written and deal with money that he sends home to his family, specific duties that he had been required to undertake, comments or requests from passengers, the important ones he seems to have underlined. There was only one reference that may have a sinister connotation. The reference in respect of 1951 and 1953 is underlined and appears to be hurried, less neat, and so Kay had asked one of her staff, DI Blanchard, to research these dates particularly in connection with the Queen. We know that the Queen's coronation was on the 2nd June, 1953 following the death of her father George VI on the

6th February, 1952, but was there something else?   We think there was, Alivia.'

'The big question was: Why should Fransesco underline the 1951 and 1953 dates on the 5th April and include the words "very angry"?' posed Mark. 'Was it to remind him of an anniversary, to carry out a task, to check on something maybe? A mistake he had made? I don't know,' he asked rhetorically. 'What we do know is that the nature of the notation was hurried with an unusual lack of neatness, as if he had written it whilst walking in a corridor or going about his duties. We now know that Fransesco removed a book from the library entitled: *England Expects*' by Dudley Pope and that Nelson's hat, emblazoned with the *chelengk,* was stolen from National Maritime Museum in 1951. And so, I can't be certain, but I believe,' said Mark, 'that I've made a really massive blunder and got this whole business completely wrong.'

'As I did. I was wrong too,' said Kay, not defensively but professionally, 'it was a logical connection and the entry in Fransesco's notebook wasn't clear.'

'I don't follow?' questioned Alivia.

'I think that the notation is not "HM" but "HN",' said Mark as he passed Fransesco's little book to Alivia. 'I thought the "M" was just a bit scrunched up at the edge of the page, but it's not. It's a "N". I now think that the inclusion of photographs of Her Majesty and the date of 1951 are not connected at all but are coincidental. Our own steward, Paulo, tells us that Fransesco was a great admirer of the Queen and was quite angry about the influence the Chinese seemed to be developing in the Solomon Islands where he was born and his family live.'

'You will have to help me here, what is the *chelengk*?' asked Alivia.

Mark opened his buff-coloured file and found his notes. 'Most pictures of Nelson show him wearing his naval hat, the brim of which would be held in place by an elaborate jewelled rosette. Normally, the rosette would be of black silk. In Nelson's case the black silk of the rosette was augmented by the *chelengk* given to Nelson by Sultan Selim the Third of Turkey after the admiral's stunning victory over the French at the Battle of the Nile in 1798.' Mark removed a picture of Nelson from his file and handed it to Alivia.

'Oh,' observed Alivia, 'this is like the portrait of Nelson in *The Globe*.'

'That's right,' agreed Mark. 'The *chelengk* consisted of over 300 diamonds with a central Ottoman star and seven perpendicular strands of precious stone representing Nelson's seven great victories that he had achieved at that time. The design of a *chelengk* would be uniquely created for a specific person or occasion and normally have adorned a turban. In Nelson's case it was his hat. Amusingly,' added Mark with a rather childish giggle, 'the central rosette could rotate by means of a clockwork mechanism.'

'And it hasn't been recovered?'

'No,' replied Mark more seriously, 'the thief was eventually arrested but not before he sold it on for just a few thousand.'

'How much would it be worth now?' asked Alivia.

'Millions,' replied Kay, 'and so I have already instructed Pippa to halt her enquiries into the Queen's schedules and to concentrate on Admiral Nelson, the theft of antiques generally and priceless jewels – something I have no knowledge of at all.

***

Pippa Blanchard did speak with Mark and Kay on the third day at sea. She would continue her enquiries but reminding them that these types of thefts constituted a multi-million pound world-wide criminal industry. Pippa gave examples of the theft in 1795 of the French royal regalia, never to be recovered. So too the theft in 1907 of the crown jewels of Ireland from Dublin Castle.

'Well, this demonstrates how little I know,' said Mark, 'I didn't even realise there had been Irish crown jewels, let alone stolen.'

'Not all the missing jewels have necessarily been stolen,' continued Pippa, 'some may have simply been lost as is the case of seven of the fifty-odd Fabergé eggs after the 1917 Russian Revolution.'

'Any idea, Pippa, of the value of an egg?' asked a curious Mark.

'Yes, anything between £10 million and £45 million.'

'Goodness and lost you say?'

'Lost or stolen as is the case of a necklace from the treasury of the Maharaja of Patiala in 1848. These thefts are the really interesting ones but the thefts are still going on today but tend not to make the headlines. One that did, but only for a day, was the theft of Viscount Montgomery's field marshal's baton when he was away from his home attending his 80th birthday party in London in 1968 and then there was Admiral Nelson's hat stolen in 1951 and never found but is believed to have changed hands recently in the States.'

There was utter silence. 'Is everything alright?' asked Pippa.

'More than alright, Pippa,' replied Faraday, 'thoughts of Nelson's hat have been tormenting me for days and now your throw-away remark that his hat may have changed hands in the US could mean that there is a connection with what's going on here. I'm not sure how or why but what you have said shows us that there is a thriving business which must be supported by a sophisticated criminal network, involving millions. With so much at stake, I think we can assume that the business will be run ruthlessly, and murder would be a regular feature of such thefts.'

***

That evening Mark and Kay joined Peter and Sarah in the *Venetian Bar* which had become one of their favourite haunts. Sarah seemed to be in mild hysterics. 'Ah,' said Sarah as she waved excitedly a photograph in her hand, 'just in time to give us your expert opinion.'

'I'm sure they would be too polite to comment,' said Peter without conviction but plenty of humour, 'it's so embarrassing.'

'No, we value their objectivity, Peter,' she insisted in mock seriousness, then turned to Mark and Kay. 'We've been to the Photo Gallery and we have discovered this less than flattering photograph of us both.' Sarah began giggling again and collapsed over her husband's shoulder. 'I look as if I am deranged and Peter looks as if he has a hang-over, or probably two. No, three. The question is: should we enter this photograph into the up-coming competition?'

'I think we should decline and allow other passengers a reasonable chance of winning,' suggested an amused Peter who then spluttered into laughter.

'Let them have a look,' said Sarah and laid the photograph on the table and pushed it towards Mark and Kay. The photograph was not very flattering, it was just a fun and an amusing shot of two people enjoying themselves in front of *'Jewels just for You from Around the World'*. In the background was Mr Featherstone standing behind his counter with the display of diamonds on the central display island which included a *Manhattan Necklace*, a necklace that hangs down and fans out and held in place by a fine silver *memory wire.* Peter and Sarah were all amused smiles. Mr Featherstone was not smiling at all, in fact he looked – uneasy. That was the word. Uneasy.

The photograph was face on to Peter and Sarah but upside down to Mark and Kay. Kay picked up the photograph, turned it around and shared it with Mark.

'Well, I think this is a winner,' said Mark to Kay as he allowed his index finger to surreptitiously point at the necklace. For a few moments Kay did not grasp the significance of what Mark was indicating. 'I would need to study it more closely,' he said, making a pretence of examining the photograph. But it wasn't a pretence.

'I think they have an unfair advantage and should be disqualified from the competition, don't you think?' said

Kay, playing her part instinctively although not realising the significance.

'Yes, I agree,' said Mark and returned the photograph to Sarah. 'We should drink to uninhibited happiness and fun, but ... um ... maybe it would be wise for the reputation and future of your company to destroy the photograph.'

There was more laughter before they went to the *Miame Atrium* and danced away the evening, their final dance being *'Let It Be Me'*, the lyrics and music by Delanoe, Becaud and Curtis beautifully sung by the *'Tranquillity Trio'* accompanied by the piano, sax and the drums gently caressed by the metal switch brushes.

Mark and Kay smooched their way around the floor to the seductive notes of the sax and the words: ... *'I bless the day'* ... *'I bless the day I found you'* ... *'without your sweet love, what would life be'* ... . They glided around the floor oblivious to others, during these tender moments no one else mattered ... *'so never leave me lonely'* ... *'say that you love me only'* ... . They continued to dance but they didn't concentrate on the perfection of their steps, there was no need, steps didn't matter ... *'and that you'll always'* ... *'let it be me.'*

***

In their stateroom Kay asked the significance of the photograph.

'The *Manhattan necklace* is a perfect inversion of Nelson's *chelengk*,' said Mark. 'The necklace on Featherstone's display has seven strands of diamonds and other semi-precious jewels. If you wanted to smuggle the *chelengk* from the US to the UK, what better way than to break it neatly down and disguised it as a modern necklace, perfectly hidden in plain sight,' suggested Mark. There was a pause. 'You look sceptical?'

'No, just thinking,' Kay said. 'Alivia says that Craddock issues some form of 'exemption' certificates for jewellery, otherwise every item of jewellery, every watch, everything would have to be itemised and possibly examined, what did she say, two-point one million pounds worth of items, literally hundreds of items. The necklace on display is housed in a perfect purpose-built velvet case. I doubt if anyone would question its background and Alivia tells us that these exemption certificates have photographs attached. It would all look innocent enough.'

'And the other items that make up the *chelengk* could be part of a collection of brooches, earrings, those sorts of items?'

'I should have thought so,' agreed Kay, 'and Featherstone didn't look too pleased in the photograph. Certainly not his usual congenial self.'

'No, he didn't look too cheerful did he,' said Mark his mind drifted. 'How much did Pippa suggest that Nelson's *chelengk* would be worth?'

'Eight to twelve million,' recalled Kay, 'but if it came up for auction in November and the anniversary of the Battle of Trafalgar, or in 2025, say on the 220 year anniversary, then probably as much as fifteen million. Just think of how much Elizabeth Taylor's jewels sold for. It might seem a lot but there again Diego Maradona's "Hand of God" World Cup shirt sold for 7.2 million. Fifteen million might be considered very reasonable, if not under-valued.'

***

They sat in their lounge and sipped their drinks, Kay a *Blue Gin*, Mark a *Macleod's* single malt whisky. They had been talking for over a half hour.

'I think there's enough, darling,' said Kay. 'You do too?'

'I think so. No direct evidence, I agree. All speculation. Reasonable speculation. But it's compelling. We know that Featherstone was boastful, then resentful when he believed that he wasn't sufficiently recognised for his clearly very ballsy action when the jeweller's shop was attacked. And the jeweller, Bessell, deals in expensive antiques and has been "a person of interest" on at least two occasions before. He would be the perfect link in any chain dealing with stolen antiques.'

'And that's a connection we can't ignore', suggested Kay. She thought for a moment, then continued. 'The death of his mother must have hurt,' added Kay, 'the family business went bust and he had the embarrassment of leaving his private school.'

'Yes, and it must have been even more than galling to wait at tables, no doubt on occasions having to wait on his ex-school chums and families,' speculated Mark.

'And we know that Fransesco Maresca was his steward who could have discovered what Featherstone was up to.'

'Fransesco must have had an inkling that Featherstone was up to something. He had been a steward for quite a time, a dozen years I think. People, and that must include Featherstone, are creatures of habit and Fransesco had been Featherstone's steward for three years. He would have sensed something. I'm speculating,' Mark suggested, 'but I had assumed the scribbled entry about being angry was all to do with the Queen. Could it not be that if Fransesco challenged Featherstone about something, maybe the jewels. Featherstone became angry, but not angry enough for a major confrontation, but enough for him to facilitate getting him out of the way?'

'He had the means to do that. We know that he had connections in every port and now we know that the *chelengk* is "doing the rounds" and believe that the

Manhattan necklace could reasonably be assumed to be part of Nelson's *chelengk.* If we were back home, we would have Featherstone in, in for questioning.'

'Okay. Let's do it,' agreed Mark.

Chapter Twenty-One

Monday, 29th April, 2019.
Eighty-seven nautical miles east of the island of Antigua, the Caribbean Sea.

KAY ANSWERED THE PHONE. 'I need to speak with you both,' said Alivia Lace, her voice full of agitation and urgency.

'Can you come to our suite now?' suggested Kay calmly.

'Five minutes.'

'Five minutes is fine.' It would be 4 minutes, 22 seconds.

She knocked on the door of 208. Mark answered. 'I've a coffee for you,' he said as he walked her through.

'Coffee would be good, I think I might need it,' she said. She appeared anxious. 'I hope I'm not jumping to silly conclusions.'

'We like silly conclusions, Alivia, which are often very sensible conclusions,' encouraged Mark. 'Take a seat and tell us what's on your mind.'

'Okay. Here goes.' She took a deep breath. 'I think the Latvians are about to jump ship.'

'Go on,' said Kay calmly, showing no surprise at all.

'Tomorrow we dock in Saint Lucia, with eight days of this voyage remaining, yet I have discovered from Reception and Accounts that the Latvians have booked a flight from Saint Lucia to the Dominican Republic. Why should they do that?'

'I wouldn't know,' replied Mark curiously. 'Did they give any reason at Reception or Accounts?

'None at all,' she replied, although that would be unusual thought Kay. Normally some remark, however small, would be made that would provide a clue to intentions.

'And so no comments about a family bereavement, an illness, meeting up with an unexpected friend, something like that?' probed Kay.

'Nothing,' Alivia replied as if her suggestion was clearly silly after all. But her reply wasn't silly although very likely inaccurate. Something would have been said.

'And so what alerted you?' questioned Kay.

'At Reception they asked for confirmation of docking and disembarkation times, although the details were already listed in the *Tranquil Times*. It just seemed an unnecessary enquiry,' replied Alivia with embarrassment, 'and one of the girls thought they seemed "jittery" but she couldn't explain why.'

And so comments were made, but Kay let that rest. 'That's okay,' said Kay, 'it's often the case that people are at a loss to understand the significance of an individual's behaviour. And at Accounts?'

'They wanted to change up their money for Dominican pesos, which didn't seem to make sense to me as US dollars are accepted virtually everywhere.'

Mark was silent in deep dream-like thought. Kay raised her hand to Alivia and moved her head from side to side to silence any comment, allowing Mark to form scenarios in his mind, some would be logical, some bizarre, some completely off the plot, precisely the reason why GCHQ actively recruit dyslexics.

'Well done, Alivia,' he said after some moments, nodding his head up and down to her immense relief. 'Very well done. You took a personal risk telling us, you could have appeared foolish but you made a decision and took a chance. Your alertness has provided us with much to think about.'

Kay nodded in agreement as Mark continued. 'The Latvians are going to act, act in some way, but absenting themselves before the consequences of their actions come to fruition. We have to quickly work out what they are up to and then act ourselves.'

A heavy silence hung in the air. Alivia was still tense. Kay thoughtful. Mark seemed to be in *evaluation* mode followed by *ready for action* mode. Then he spoke. 'We need to have a meeting with Captain Dunbar most immediate. Can you arrange that, Alivia?'

'I think so.'

'We are way past thinking, Alivia, I'm relying on you to do so. Let me explain what I think is going down here.'

***

Mark, Kay and Alivia discussed Mark's assessment. Kay agreed with his conclusions. Alivia was shocked. Alivia had more coffee. Strong coffee. Alivia needed it. Alivia rang Craddock and asked to be excused from her afternoon duties as she didn't feel too well. This wasn't a lie. Far from it. Mark's assessment didn't make her feel too good at all and she remained in 208 for a few hours to allow some calmness to return. It was a *defence* mechanism of course, but such mechanisms can prove useful as they provide an individual time to solve issues that might otherwise overwhelm them. And so it proved to be. Alivia reflected on her OTC training and on many of the stories her father had shared with her which brought about a change of perspective and a determination to play her part.

***

They were seated in the Captain's cabin around a small conference table. Mark Faraday, Kay Yin, Alivia Lace and Craddock. It was late evening and all business. There was an air of anticipation. The cabin was essentially a passenger stateroom with the lounge area converted to an office with telephone handsets on the wall above a desk and navigation and data repeater screens to the side. The captain, Captain Robert Dunbar, took his seat behind his desk, his left hand wedged into the crux of his right elbow, his right hand across his mouth. He was in a pensive – no, that wasn't it, he was in *challenging* mode. Not the most welcoming of starts.

'Captain, thank you for seeing us at such short notice,' said Mark.

'You said it was urgent, very urgent and involved the safety of my ship,' he replied, a certain abruptness in his tone.

'And so let me get straight to the point as time is of the essence here,' said Mark. Captain Dunbar was about to speak but Mark closed him down with a hand gesture. Captain Dunbar folded his arms, Mark's gesture clearly resented.

'Your ship, Captain, your ship is in grave danger as are the one thousand eight hundred and fifty-nine souls on board.' It was a stark warning as intended. 'I am not one to exaggerate. Like you I have heavy responsibilities as the police commander of the whole of the city of Bristol with its population of nearly four-hundred thousand,' continued Mark without arrogance but partly to emphasise his role and responsibilities which also gave him the opportunity to indicate his experience, 'a city that has had its encounters with terrorists, mainly the IRA of course but other groups too. More importantly, I was at one stage the head of the force's Special Branch. By coincidence my wife here is a Detective Superintendent and now heads Special Branch herself,' a revelation that took Captain Dunbar by surprise, his resentment replaced by concern as Mark continued, 'consequently, we both have significant experience of assessing terrorist threats and dealing with terrorists. By way of observations, and from enquiries here on board and back home we now know that two of your passengers, Mr and Mrs Heckhausen from Latvia, are not who they purport to be. Worryingly, Mr Heckhausen is in fact Oleg Sukhovetsky an agent of the Russian intelligence service, the FSB, formerly known as the KGB, the agency responsible for the Novichok attack in Salisbury during 2018 and the attack upon Alexei Navalny two years later.'

Captain Dunbar's posture changed, as did his facial countenance to one of intense interest, expressing much greater, if not grave concern. Cleary, they had his attention now.

'The Heckhausens,' said Kay, an intervention intended to demonstrate that both officers were on exactly the same page, 'were supposed to travel on to Southampton. We now know, through the excellent work of your Deputy

Chief here, that the Heckhausens have booked a 12.16pm flight from Saint Lucia to the Dominican Republic's Punta Cana airport. Why should that be?' Kay asked rhetorically. 'We believe that they plan to contaminate your ship, possibly with Novichok, Carentanyl or maybe Sarin.' Kay and Mark deliberately paused and allowed the captain to absorb the significance of this information and the opportunity for a question.

'How is this terrorist act to be perpetrated? asked Captain Dunbar seriously.

'By way of a Jack-in-the Box,' replied Mark his expression full of seriousness.

'A Jack-in-the Box?' asked the captain, not sure whether to be shocked, angry or amused.

'Yes. I am sure that such a toy with an electric timer will be used to activate a toxic contamination,' replied Mark.

'I'm sorry. Are you really being serious?' he demanded, irritation in his tone.

But the choice to speak of the 'jack in the box' was intentional. Mark and Kay were not going to engage in BS. They would be truthful and transparent and, in doing so, hoped to convince Captain Dunbar of their seriousness.

'We are always serious, Captain,' interjected Kay, 'as you must be when in command of the *Tranquillity*.' She paused, her no-nonsense stare penetrating before continuing. 'A terrorist agent can hardly bring on board a ship that caters for a passenger's ever need an alarm clock and other paraphernalia useful to perpetrate a terrorist attack. If the toxins are contained in perfume bottles, which we suspect they are and easy enough to bring through a baggage inspection, there must be a means to break them open when required whilst not endangering their agents. Dropping from a height on to a solid ceramic wash hand basin or bath or shower unit would be idea, once of course the Heckhausens had vacated their stateroom. When Housekeeping opens their door it would be impossible to contain the toxin.'

'And you know the mechanism to be used to achieve this contamination is this Jack-in-the Box?' he asked of Mark, ignoring Kay.

'Pretty certain,' replied Kay.

'Only "pretty certain" you say?' he questioned with a tinge of smug annoyance.

'Like the command of a ship,' countered Kay, 'nothing is certain at sea which can, as you know, be an *unforgiving* environment.' Kay deliberately used the word 'unforgiving' and she and Mark would use and emphasise similar adjectives during their conversation to remind the captain of his potential vulnerability and responsibilities should a catastrophe engulf his ship.

'And you saw the Heckhausens obtain this Jack-in-the Box?'

'Yes,' replied Mark, 'as did Professor Bodkin, a fellow passenger.'

Captain Dunbar swiftly ran his fingers over his desk computer screen. He found her sailing details. 'Professor Bodkin is a 77-year-old pensioner?' he queried as if her judgement would automatically be in doubt.

'Yes, but her age doesn't mean that she is an imbecile,' said Kay calmly. 'We have become acquainted with her and it is true that she often pretends to be a rather dotty professor of psychology which she is, a professor of criminal psychology in fact, not dotty, and she also continues to act as a highly regarded police consultant in people profiling and an expert witness for the Crown.

'Maybe I'm being a little naïve, but why please tell me should Russia want to attack my ship?' he asked, posing his question to Mark.

'I don't think you are being naïve at all,' replied Kay. 'In fact I'm surprised that something of this sort hasn't happened before. There are plenty of isolated attacks across the world all the time and some very spectacular ones. I suppose we can go back to the Palestinian hijacking and subsequent destruction of four passenger aircraft at Dawson Field, a former RAF base, way back in Jordan during 1970 was a notable one which resulted in dramatic headlines of aircraft being blown up. The more recent disappearance of Malaysia Airline Flight 370 in 2014 with the loss of 227 passengers and 12 crew, and then the loss of another Malaysian airliner, Flight 17, brought down by a missile over conflict-stricken Ukraine are examples of the publicity that these events attract and generate. Whether they are terrorist related or blackmail, pilot error or mechanical failure or designed to demonstrate the vulnerability or failure of governments to protect their own people is not clear. What is clear is the subsequent publicity. The image of a cruise liner adrift on the high seas for months on end filled with the dead and dying would be a horrific spectacle.'

'I note what your colleague is saying, Mr Faraday ... ,' rudely ignoring Kay again.

Mark, by now clearly annoyed interrupted Captain Dunbar. 'Captain, Miss Yin is my colleague, but she is also my wife. I would be very much obliged if you did not dismiss and disrespect her. I think you will find it useful to hear what she has to say.'

'My apologies, but you will excuse me if I am being sceptical. I'm visualising the newspaper headlines, me portrayed in a cartoon as the Jack-in-the-Box alongside a very angry Russian ambassador.'

'I believe there is a more likely and *attractive* alternative for *you* to consider, Captain,' responded Kay.

'Well I can't wait to hear of it,' he said as he leaned forward across his desk, the fingers of his hands intertwined his head slightly to one side, a *questioning* pose, making no attempt to disguise his impatience.

'We were thinking,' offered Kay, 'more of you being portrayed as a latter-day Captain Kendall or Captain Rostron, not a hapless Captain Lord. The choice of course would be yours.' Kay paused to allow the implication of the names of Kendall, Rostron and Lord to register with Captain Dunbar whose impatience was almost instantly replaced by an acknowledgement and intense curiosity as to how this scenario could be one transformed to his advantage.

'These names will be familiar to you, Captain, of course,' said Mark, 'but, for the benefit of Miss Lace and Mr Craddock you will know that in 1910 Captain Henry Kendall, Master of the *SS Montrose* was *pretty* certain that one of his passengers travelling to the States was Dr Crippen who was wanted for the murder of his wife Cora. Although Crippen had shaved off his moustache and was accompanied by a "boy", Captain Kendall judged "him" to be a female due to manner, build and gait. He very *wisely* contacted his head office who in turn contacted Scotland Yard who dispatched Chief Inspector Dew to Liverpool. The policeman boarded the much faster *SS Laurentic*, overtook the *Montrose* and arrested Dr Crippen and the "boy" who transpired to be his lover, Ethel Le Neve. As is so often the case the obsessed self-destruct and Crippen was subsequently hanged in Pentonville Prison for the murder of his wife.'

'Probably very much more significantly,' suggested Kay, 'was the *casual* conduct of Captain Stanley Lord, Master of the *SS California,* who in 1912 was informed of the distress signals from the *Titanic*. He chose to ignore the signals but Captain Arthur Rostron of the *RMS Carpathia* did not. The, how shall I describe him, yes, the *bold* and determined Captain Rostron steamed at full speed, in fact much faster than his ship's recommended top speed of 17.5 knots, for more than three hours through the ice packs and rescued 705 of *Titanic's* passengers whilst Captain Lord did nothing and, ah yes, I remember now, went back to sleep in his cabin.'

Captain Dunbar was hesitant, he still had in his mind the thoughts of his portrayal in a newspaper's cartoon. But he was also used to women being in awe of him and he did not take to the assertive Chinese detective's no-nonsense approach whom he viewed as an over confident up-start with few responsibilities, who probably achieved her position as a result of her husband, but he acknowledged that she would very likely make a formidable and compelling witness in any future enquiry. Her precise and direct comments were delivered in a manner, as was her intention, that left him little room for manoeuvre. 'You will I'm sure recall,' continued Kay pointedly, her countenance hardened, 'that Captain Lord was subsequently subject to considerable criticism by the Board of Enquiry. Captain Arthur Rostron was subsequently knighted.'

The implications of what Mark and Kay had said were not lost on Captain Dunbar. He thought for a moment longer – well, a very short moment longer.

'You have a plan, I suppose?' he asked.

'Of course,' replied Mark and Kay in unison.

Chapter Twenty-Two

Tuesday, 30th April, 2019.
Sixteen nautical miles east of the island of
Antigua, the Caribbean Sea.

IT WAS 3.45am LOCAL TIME PRECISELY. At each end of the port-side corridor on Deck 8 was stationed a member of the ship's security team. Outside of the Heckhausen's stateroom to the left were Deputy Chief of Security Alivia Lace and Kay Yin. To the right, Shane Wood and Mark Faraday. Across the corridor and directly opposite Heckhausen's stateroom was a rather pensive Craddock.

Alivia Lace held her master key to the Heckhausen's door. A little green light flickered in response. The door unlocked.

There was the silence of anticipation. You could feel it. You could touch it. An intense silence that enveloped them all.

Mark edged open the door - only sufficiently so as to confirm which side of the king-sized bed the occupants lay. Conveniently, the male was to the right. The female to the left.

Mark paused for a short moment, looked at each of the team in turn indicating the Heckhausens' disposition. They nodded in return. Satisfied that they were ready he pushed the door open wide. Instantly Shane Wood launched himself upon Mr Heckhausen. Heckhausen tumbled to the hard floor without ceremony. As intended. The wind was knocked from his chest. As intended. Shock immobilised him as both Shane and Mark secured his wrists with plastic ties.

'Be absolutely quiet and still and we won't hurt you,' whispered Mark into Heckhausen's ear. It wasn't 'you won't get hurt', it was 'we won't hurt you.' A very clear and no-nonsense threat of the final sanction, pain, if he failed to comply. He got the message.

At the same moment, Kay and Alivia had bundled Mrs Heckhausen to the floor. Shocked, she looked for a moment terrified as she was roughly turned onto her front and her wrists secured.

Simultaneously the stateroom door had closed and lights turned on, actions that were perfectly co-ordinated, with two female uniformed security staff now standing inside at the door. The whole operation took seventeen seconds. As previously arranged, the security staff together with Alivia and Kay, Mark and Shane, hauled the Latvian pair up and onto the bed.

'Listen carefully to what I have to say,' said Alivia Lace dressed in her pristine white uniform. 'I am detaining you both under the provisions of Section 12 of the Aviation and Maritime Security Act.'

The Latvians exchanged glances. They were dumb founded. Shocked. Incapable of formulating a response.

Whilst Alivia oversaw the detention of the Latvians, Mark and Kay began their search. The first object of their attention was the safe inside the wardrobe. 'The number?' demanded Mark without ceremony.

'6844,' blurted Mr Heckhausen without hesitation, maybe conscious of how Russian agents would ordinarily operate and the painful consequences of any failure to comply with a similar request.

Kay tapped in the numbers on the door of the safe. There was a whirling sound followed by a distinctive click. Kay carefully opened the safe door to its full extent, shone her torch inside to reveal two mobile phones, a small notebook and two glass phials of liquid, each the size of a lipstick, in a perfume-style presentation box. Kay took a photograph on her mobile phone of the safe's interior, then another close-up of the phials. She then removed the mobile phones and notebook and shut and locked the safe door. As agreed, Kay nodded to Alivia.

'I have reason to believe,' said Deputy Chief of Security Alivia Lace formally, remembering the correct phraseology she had rehearsed with Mark and Kay, 'that you intended to seriously interfere with the operation of this ship and, on behalf of the ship's Master, you are detained and will be delivered to a police officer when we dock in Southampton.' Mr and Mrs Heckhausen said nothing but lowered their heads as if in defeat.

Now the wider and methodical search began of drawers, cupboards, suitcases, travel and toiletry bags, shoes and clothing, including the 'jack in the box', the *Cellotape* fixed to the top of shower cubicle ready for the two glass phials. In fact, everything and everywhere. The search would take nearly two hours. A few letters were found, a family photograph, credit cards – all would prove useful when examined. The existence of the notebook and two mobile phones was sloppy and would be of value to investigators.

At 7.30am Mr and Mrs Croker, the occupants of the inside stateroom directly across the corridor and immediately opposite the Heckhausens vacated their accommodation and were delighted to be 'promoted' to a much superior balcony stateroom on Deck 9. The Croker's stateroom door was left ajar and occupied by one of the security staff, thus negating the necessity of having a guard conspicuously stationed in the corridor. Three security staff remained with the Heckhausens 24/7. Once they had recovered from the manner of their detention, they both complained of their rough handling which they described as 'brutal', the indignity of the toilet arrangements and the lack of choice for meals but, eventually, they settled into a routine as they accepted the inevitable, their fate.

***

Captain Dunbar was pleased and relieved at the outcome of the operation. He was reassured by Mark's draft report, a report that would not result in a knighthood but would certainly attract praise. In fact, everyone involved in the operation had cause to be pleased – other than the Heckhausens. What was believed to be deadly and toxic chemicals had been identified and secured. The crew and passengers, all 1,559 of them, were safe too. The passengers and crew, with the exception of those involved in the operation, were oblivious to the action. The cruise would continue without panic or disruption. The cruise company's headquarters were already formulating a positive and reassuring press statement that would be presented with edits - 'when appropriate' of course - in conjunction with the National Crime Agency although the Home Office and the Foreign and Commonwealth Office would bicker over who should take the lead at any press conference that would inevitably follow.

The NCA had been quickly informed of the operation and valuable information would later be gleaned from the Heckhausens and their notebook and phones. For the moment, the identity and detention of the Heckhausens would remain secret and the Russian intelligence service would be confused for a time as to exactly what had happened - was the delay the result of total failure or simply a prudent rearrangement of their operation by the Heckhausens? The Heckhausens were already seeking a deal and asylum, although this disloyalty to Mother Russia would be greeted with a terrible vengeance as was the case of Sergei Skripal, Anna Politkovskaya and so many others.

Mark and Kay anticipated criticism of their actions when they reached the UK by those in the comfort of their offices, some of whom would say that the *Tranquillity* should have sailed to Bermuda where the ship should have remained and subjected to a full-scale decontamination protocol. This had been considered by Mark and Kay but this wasn't really feasible. There was no pressing need for that, even if major and sophisticated local facilities had been readily available. Critically, there was no known exposure and careful judgement and swift and covert action had been the order of the day. The action on board the ship did not jeopardize any current or future NCA operations and everyone was safe. That was all that really mattered.

A little after 8am Mark lay on their bed with Kay. She knelt up and placed her knees each side of his chest. His heartbeat increased but she put an index finger to his lips. 'You are deep in thought again,' she said gently. 'What is it? Tell me?'

He smiled. 'I've been thinking of Detective Chief Inspector Walter Dew and his arrest of Doctor Crippen. Did you know that Dew was also something of an expert in respect of the thefts of jewellery and antiques? I'm just thinking that, maybe, we should now focus on the murder of Fransesco Maresca.'

***

They had had only four hours sleep and so took an early lunch. That said, Mark and Kay were also keen to act as normal passengers and went ashore. Antigua boasts a beach for every day of the year, each of which had seas that sparkle in every shade of blue. They swam, swam close, but mostly in silent reflection, then walked hand-in-hand around English Harbour and the Georgian *Nelson's Dockyard* that had been carefully restored or repaired over the years.

Begun in 1725, Nelson was first stationed there in 1784 where he met Francis, the 'pretty and sensible' widow of Dr Josiah Nisbet whom he married three years later. The site included the Captain's House, the Mast House and Blacksmith's forge, the Engineer's House and Copper, Canvas and Lumber Stores, the Old Bakery and the quarters for officers and men, now the main gift shop which they intended to visit. But they did not enter. They saw that Featherstone was already there engrossed in the extensive collection of Nelson-inspired books.

Instinctively and without discussion, Mark and Kay wanted Featherstone to see them so they stood at the shop's window and simply scanned the contents on display. Featherstone eventually turned and saw them. They exchanged acknowledgements. Featherstone looked unsettled rubbing the back of his neck with his free hand, a gesture of frustration and agitation. He fumbled with the book in his other hand, looked at the book cover and returned it to the shelf. Sensibly, he quickly evaluated the position in which he found himself. He reasoned logically that he should act in an unhurried and natural way. As a result his body language changed as he regained his composure and selected another book the index of which he examined carefully in a display of suppression of any impulse to panic and draw attention to himself whilst Mark and Kay looked towards him with mild disinterest.

They both continued to scan the window display, pointing at various items then walked on. Featherstone smirked in relief, confident that any interest the two police officers had in him or Nelson would be fleeting and nugatory. But that would suit the officers perfectly. He would drop his guard with arrogance leading to carelessness. That had been their quick-thinking intention.

Back on board, the afternoon was taken up with an American-styled BBQ of Porterhouse and Rump steaks, T-bone and Scotch Fillets, with sweet potatoes, fried rice, *calabacta*, lemon garlic broccoli, honey-glazed baby potatoes and a tasty concoction of peas, mushrooms and onions – and much more, all eaten against a background of Country and Western music performed by the gifted and versatile *Tranquillity Trio* including *'I Walked the Line'* made famous by Johnny Cash, and *'Rhinestone Cowboy'* and *'Wichita Cowboy'* by Glen Campbell. Female singers featured too, applauded by enthusiastic clapping when the *Trio* performed songs which included *'Don't It Make*

My Brown Eyes Blue' by Crystal Gale and Dolly Parton's *'Jolene'*.

Chapter Twenty-Three

Friday, 3rd May, 2019.
The British Overseas Territory, Bermuda, the North Atlantic Ocean.

'STEP BACK PLEASE, SIR, WE NEED TO SEARCH YOUR CABIN,' said Detective Superintendent Kay Yin to Gerald Featherstone who opened his cabin door at 2.30am still wearing his rather gaudy and crumpled pyjamas. He was full of panic, the seriousness of Kay's words confirmed by the ominous presence of a Chief Inspector of the Bermuda Police Service.

'Is this some sort of joke, Mrs Faraday?' he said feigning innocence, but his eyes betrayed him. His pupils dilated.

'Certainly not,' she replied, not in a serious tone or one to humiliate him but in her usual disarming style that would confuse a suspect who would wonder whether this officer was unreal, casual or to be wary of. It would be wise for anyone to be very wary. 'Please step back,' her tone much more direct and firm. Featherstone backed into his stateroom followed by Mark, Kay and the policeman. They closed the door. Kay spoke again. 'Meanwhile let me make it clear to you that you are now under arrest in connection with the murder of Fransesco Maresca between the 11th and 12th of April, 2012 in Mexico.'

His pupils dilated even more under the strong emotion of these words that brought back to him the part that he had played in the death of Fransesco Maresca. And so he sought to minimise any connection he had with the victim.

'He was just a steward. I didn't have time to get to know him at all,' he said defensively, then blustered foolishly, 'Anyway, you can't arrest me for a murder in Mexico,' as if these words would confirm in his mind what he had already confidently considered.

'I think you will find that I can and I just have,' replied Kay in that unreal and casual tone which, nevertheless, was full of menace. 'You see, Mr Featherstone, the Offences Against the Persons Act 1861 as amended by the Criminal Law Act 1977 is quite clear. Complicity in a murder by one of Her Majesty's subjects,' she paused and smiled, 'ah, and that's you, of anyone, and that's Fransesco Maresca, anywhere in the world can be "inquired into, tried and punished" as if committed in the United Kingdom.'

These facts put so succinctly and confidently by this senior detective muddled his thought processes, resulted in a poorly considered response, 'I haven't murdered anyone,' he replied as if such a suggestion that he would actually murder anyone was preposterous. A classic *denial* response. But Kay had not said that he 'had murdered' anyone, merely that he was arrested for being 'connected' with the murder, or 'complicity'.

'That's the unenviable position you find yourself in, Mr Featherstone,' she said with a confident smile, 'you see you don't actually have to commit the murder yourself, arranging for it to be carried out will do quite nicely.'

'But what about my things,' he demanded - a classic *suppression* response.

'Ah, yes, your things,' she said as if his personal possessions had slipped her mind. 'Like you, they will be coming with us. Miss Lace will supervise you packing two cases, one appropriate for a day trip, another for a week. The remainder of your property, excluding matters of evidential significance, will be seized and freight shipped to the Hampshire's police headquarters later.'

Featherstone said nothing but, after Kay had used the words 'your property' Featherstone could not disguise the slightest of smirks indicating, for a pico-second, a renewed confidence. Mistake. Why? All a matter of body language. Nothing went unnoticed by Kay and there must have been a reason for Featherstone's smirk. One reason immediately came to mind and as a result Kay would ensure that Alivia Lace undertook a thorough search of Stephanie Ash's cabin, the young lady they believed to be Featherstone's on-board girlfriend.

Photographs of Featherstone's cabin were taken. Alivia Lace oversaw the packing as Featherstone advised as to what he thought he would need. But he did so in an agitated way, not sure as to what clothing he would in reality require whilst constantly distracted by what items Mark and Kay were bagging, tagging and recording on a clipboard. His body language was classic *disapproval* mixed with nervousness and maybe even fear, impossible for him to disguise and recorded meticulously by Mark.

A nine-seater RAF Hawker Beachcraft B200, in the colours and registration of a civilian company, *Executive Air*, was standing-by at St George's, formally part of the US Naval Air Station, awaiting the arrival of the Heckhausens, Featherstone, Mark and Kay.

The *Tranquillity* had docked at Hamilton a little after ten past four. Mark and Kay had finished examining Featherstone's cabin, examined the Security Locker and *'Jewels for You from Around the World'* concession and by 5.30am Faraday's party were on their way to the airport. At the airport Kay briefed two British CSIs and two scientific officers from the Defence Science Technology Laboratory at Porton Down, Wiltshire who had arrive on the Hawker Beachcraft.

Now Mark and Kay settled for the seven-hour flight. The Heckhausens shuffled about in their seats, irritated that they should each be handcuffed to their arm rests by one wrist. But they quite quickly settled until meals were served one hour into the flight. Probably their Russian secret service training began to come into play and they were already prepared for what was to come. Mark and Kay paid them little attention. Their case would be handled by Scotland Yard and MI5. Not so with

Featherstone. His case, in agreement with the Hampshire Constabulary would be handled by Mark and Kay, with support from Scotland Yard's Arts and Antiques Unit. Featherstone had no record or experience of arrest. He could only guess at what was to come. His preparation would undoubtably be shallow. That said, Featherstone was no fool, he was educated and intelligent and would be fighting for his freedom.

Nevertheless, Featherstone was agitated throughout the flight. He picked at his food and ate little although drank a great deal of coffee and water. In between his constant trips to the toilet, accompanied by Mark, he would regularly look across the facing seats towards Mark and Kay – particularly Kay for whom he would regularly fantasise. A recurring fantasy was the hope that he would be interviewed by Kay. His hope would be fulfilled but regretted. In his deluded mind he imagined that Kay would absolve him from any responsibility for the death of the steward. And so, throughout the flight, his demeanour ranged from sheepish to agitated, thoughtful and immensely hopeful.

They landed at RAF Brize Norton. The Heckhausens were taken to London in separate Special Branch Jaguars, escorted by three Special Branch Audis, whilst Featherstone was taken to police headquarters at Eastleigh in a Ford Transit van.

Chapter Twenty-Four

Saturday, 4ᵗʰ May, 2019.
Hampshire Constabulary Headquarters, Eastleigh,
Hampshire, England.

AT 10am THEY ENTERED INTERVIEW ROOM 7. Featherstone and his solicitor, Sullivan, were already present, seated behind a grey metal table, facing the door.

'Good morning, Mr Sullivan, Mr Featherstone,' said Faraday as he pulled out a chair for Kay to sit down to his left. Sullivan and Featherstone remained seated. Kay was wearing a very neat black trouser suit and white, open neck blouse. She placed her brief case at the left side of her chair. Mark wore a dark grey business suit and joined Kay taking a seat to her right. Mark placed his brief case flat on the table in front of himself, clicked open the twin locks and removed a blue ring binder together with a brown file and a secretary's style note book. Kay removed a red ring binder file from her briefcase. For a moment Featherstone wondered if the colours were of any significance. 'For the purpose of the tape and to aid the identification of those speaking, I am Chief Superintendent Mark Faraday and … '

'I am Detective Superintendent Kay Yin.' Mark looked across the table.

Featherstone spoke first. 'I am Gerald Featherstone.'

'Thank you, Mr Featherstone,' said Faraday, then looked towards Sullivan.

'I am Colin Sullivan, solicitor, and I represent my client, Mr Featherstone. In that capacity I have to advise you that my client will not be answering any questions put to him. However, the reasons for his arrest and detention are not clear and we would now require a much fuller explanation to be given.'

'Your comments are noted, Mr Sullivan,' replied Faraday, 'and we are now in a position to disclose greater details for you, however, we *will* be putting questions to your client ... ,' insisted Faraday.

'And my client's responses to any questions put to him will be "no comment".'

'That is his prerogative, Mr Sullivan, but Miss Yin will have questions that she *will* be asking your client ... '

'I thought I have made it very clear that my client has no comments to make.'

'But I do have questions I wish to put to your client,' said Kay. 'If he wishes to say "no comment" that is a matter for him, however, I ... '

'I have already made our ... ,' Sullivan began aggressively.

'Please do not overtalk me, Mr Sullivan, it's not really very good manners,' commented Kay knowing full well that the whole interview might be heard or a transcript read by a Crown Court jury. 'I have some new information that I am able to disclose to you and I *will* be putting questions to your client. Some of the answers he gives me may be advantageous to him particularly if they offer a quite reasonable explanation for his conduct or give us a much more productive line of enquiry or an opportunity for me to clarify some points. If your client does not wish to answer my questions, then so be it.' Kay looked towards Featherstone. 'And so, Mr Featherstone, you have a jewellery concession on board the cruise ship *Tranquillity*?'

'Yes.'

'And you trade under the name of "*Jewels for You from Around the World*".'

'That is correct.'

'And you have held this concession for three years I believe?'

'Yes.'

'Part of that concession is the provision by the ship's company of a series of drawer-like lockers in the ship's vault, which is situated in the ship's Security Locker, a facility the size of a suite?'

'Yes.'

'Who has key cards to the vault?'

'No comment.'

'Well, the Chief of Security will say that you were only one of four members of the crew issued with a key card, the operation of which is logged on a on-board computer. More importantly you were issued with a number of secure drawer-like lockers and their mortice keys situated within the vault.'

'No comment.'

'We searched one of these drawers and removed a slim, grey steel briefcase that contained a velvet triangular shaped presentation box. I am now showing Mr Featherstone Exhibit KY 63.' Kay paused. 'You know of this box. Can you tell me what it contained?'

'No comment.'

'Well, we know what it contained, as surely must you.'

'As my client has said, he has no comment to make.'

'Well, Mr Sullivan,' said Kay, 'we believe it contained a necklace in the style of what is known as a *Manhattan necklace*. For the benefit of Mr Sullivan, a *Manhattan necklace* is suspended from a solid circle of silver or gold around the neck from which hangs a series of jewelled strands fanning out and held in place by what is known as a very fine "memory wire". Our contention is that this necklace was crafted from an ornate piece of jewellery known as a *chelengk* that had been presented to Admiral Lord Nelson by Sultan Selim of Turkey after, what many consider, Nelson's greatest victory over the French at the Battle of the Nile in 1798.'

'No comment.'

'This box was essentially empty with the exception of some small pieces of jewellery from the main Turkish piece,' suggested Kay. 'As you were the only person who had a key to this drawer, can you explain how this could be?'

'No comment.'

'I am now showing Mr Featherstone Exhibit KY 66, a photograph of Mr Featherstone's concession depicting clearly the central island display which includes the *Manhattan necklace*. That is a *Manhattan necklace* is it not Mr Featherstone?'

'No comment.'

'Our contention is that this very splendid diamond display includes the component parts of Admiral Nelson's *chelengk*. Is that not so Mr Featherstone?'

'No comment.'

'The *Manhattan necklace* does not contain all of Nelson's *chelengk*. As I have already said, small items were found in the case in your secure locker, others were found in other display cabinets which can be seen in Exhibits KY 67, 68, 69, 70, 72, 74 and 76.' Kay removed a A4 envelope from her case and carefully selected seven photographs from within which she fanned out in front of Featherstone and Sullivan like a skilled croupier.

Featherstone stared at the photographs but simply replied: 'No comment.'

'But this splendid display is in *your* concession, Mr Featherstone, and it is *your* display that would have been arranged by *you*.'

'No comment.'

'You seem to be mystified as if the existence of the display is new to you. Maybe I can refresh your memory regarding the *Manhattan necklace*.'

Kay pressed a buzzer on the desk. A robotic voice answered. 'DS Monk.'

'Sergeant Monk please bring in Exhibit KY 48 please.'

Featherstone began to bite his lower lip during the short delay before Sergeant Geoffrey Monk entered, a side arm at his belt, carrying the exhibit, a velvet box, in front of him. The sergeant placed the box on the grey table. 'Don't leave, Sergeant. Remain at the door please,' said Kay deliberately adding to the tension.

'Is the presence of an armed policeman really necessary?' Is this another tactic of intimidation, Superintendent?' questioned Sullivan.

'Please be patient, Mr Sullivan. I think you will see why it is so necessary.'

Kay then carefully fingered the two clips on each side of the box and opened it carefully. As the lid was slowly raised the base of the box appeared to be empty, but as the lid rose to the perpendicular the jewels themselves were shown to be displayed on the underside of the lid in all their magnificence.

The facial expressions of Kay and Mark were quite passive whilst Featherstone's was one of well controlled frustration and annoyance. They had seen it all before of course, but Sullivan had not. His mouth simply fell open. He was speechless as he viewed the seven strands containing 300 dazzling diamonds.

'Shortly, this necklace will be taken to London,' explained Kay, 'under armed escort.   I am confident that the London experts will confirm that these jewels constitute Admiral Nelson's *chelengk* and valued conservatively at between eight and ten million pounds.'

'No comment.'

'Mr Featherstone, we know that the potential availability to thieves and smugglers of this jewellery has been "doing the rounds" in the United States for some time and has been on display on board ship since the 4th April. This jewellery is not something that you pick up at a Saturday Boot Sale or a village market.' Kay pointed to the case which distracted, as she intended, Featherstone from remembering that the investigation primarily concerned the murder of Fransesco Maresca.

'How much were you paid to transport this to the UK?' she asked.

Illogical as it seemed, an obsessed and deluded Featherstone needed to impress Kay and without any measured thought replied: 'Thirty thousand pounds. I was given fifteen thousand in Vancouver and was to receive a further fifteen on completion.'

'And that would take place where,' she asked full of interest as if a fellow conspirator, 'on completion that is?'

'At the Lord Bute Hotel in Christchurch,' he replied rather smugly still needing to impress Kay as he referred to a five-star boutique hotel. 'A suite has already been reserved for me and I was to meet a contact there,' he said to emphasise that he wasn't meeting some sort of spiv in a grubby back street.

A slight smile continued to crease Featherstone's face as he was reminded of the audacity of his involvement which he imagined had impressed Kay. But not so Mr Sullivan who raised his eyebrows in despair.

'Superintendent, I would now like to speak with my client alone,' he said, 'in order that he can make a prepared statement.'

Chapter Twenty-Five

Monday, 6th May April. 2019.
Hampshire Constabulary Headquarters, Eastleigh, England.

THE MAGISTRATES HAD APPROVED Featherstone's continued police detention. Sullivan and Featherstone were seated in the Interview Room as on Friday with Mark and Kay. Kay reiterated the legal preliminaries as before then spoke.

'On Friday,' reminded Kay, 'you admitted to us that your role in respect of the *chelengk* was essentially to act as a courier, to receive this stolen item disguised as a necklace and take it to England to be passed on to another.'

'My client agreed to his part in this matter,' interrupted a frustrated Sullivan but keen to remind any jury of his client's helpfulness. 'I'm not sure why it is necessary to go over this again after his fulsome cooperation?'

'There was some question, Mr Sullivan,' said Kay reasonably, 'regarding the authenticity and provenance of the *chelengk*. I am now able to tell you that the Institute of Professional Goldsmiths, who have received detailed photographs from us, will most certainly certify as to its authenticity as a result of their close examination of its artistry and craftmanship and the provenance will be further supported by an analysis of the gold used in other *chelengks* of a similar period. I am certain that the Institute will be able to analyse the chemical properties of the gold used and will identify the presence of *epithermal porphyry* which will confirm their preliminary view that the gold would have its origins in Çöpler in the Erzincan province of Turkey.'

'But speculation at this time,' Sullivan observed.

'"At this time". That is absolutely correct, Mr Sullivan, but I have had a team back in Bristol working around the clock and I can tell you that from their general enquiries and from specific written historical records from the Court of the Sultan, there is little doubt as to the provenance and I have taken this opportunity to give you early notice of this matter.' Sullivan eagerly scribbled notes on a pad, although this revelation was simply an interesting distraction before Kay moved on to the most critical aspect of her questioning.

'Your contention yesterday, Mr Featherstone, was that you had no intention of stealing the *chelengk*, merely carry it for another?' asked Kay.

'That is my client's position,' offered Sullivan.

'Would you care to speculate as to the value of the *chelengk*, Mr Featherstone. I understand that you thought that eight to ten million pounds would not be unreasonable?'

Sullivan did not intervene, curious to have confirmation of its value.

'I would have thought that to be quite reasonable,' replied Featherstone in a rather superior tone, pleased to be associated with an item of such value.

'Yet you were prepared to accept … ', Kay pretended to have forgotten a figure, Mark leafed through the papers in front of him, selected one sheet, the prepared statement, and pointed to a figure … 'yes, here we are, you were prepared to accept £30,000 as a fee for bringing the *chelengk* to the UK. Were you not tempted to steal the *chelengk*?'

'I'm not sure where this line of questioning is taken us, Superintendent?' asked Sullivan.

'It's taking us to the motive behind the murder of Fransesco Maresca,' suggested Kay.

Featherstone was slightly taken aback by this sudden change of direction, as was Sullivan, but Featherstone had anticipated such a question and had an answer already formulated in his mind. 'Why should I want to murder him?' asked Featherstone confidently, a smile creasing his face.

'The usual, Mr Featherstone. The usual,' she paused for effect, 'money, greed and in *your* case … resentment.'

'This is a nonsense,' he replied looking at Sullivan, Mark and Kay in turn as if shocked, adding dismissively, 'I hardly knew this steward, how was I supposed to be resentful of him?'

'You hardly knew him you say. Maybe this picture of Fransesco will jog your memory,' she said and leaned over to her left and removed a staff photograph of a smiling Fransesco from her briefcase and placed it on the table, turning it over and around so as to face Featherstone.

'I am now showing Mr Featherstone Exhibit KY 14.' Kay left the photograph on the table for a few moments to allow Featherstone to remember the once smiling and happy steward.

'I'm sure he was a pleasant and hard working enough young man,' he answered in a condescending tone, 'but otherwise I can make no useful comment.'

'Maybe this photograph, Exhibit KY 89, will indicate to you why we are so keen to understand why a lowly steward should be murdered.' Kay leaned over again and removed the exhibit from her briefcase. As she did so the emerald stone of her necklace could be seen just above her collar bone moving across her olive-coloured skin to her left only to return to the vertical as she sat up straight again. Featherstone's pulse rate increased, distracted by her beauty. He swallowed hard. He swallowed even harder as Kay laid the second photograph on the table face down and then turned it over. This second photograph depicted the twisted body of Fransesco Maresca in a shallow, dusty grave with his throat savagely cut.

'I object strongly, Detective,' said Sullivan angrily, 'producing this photograph, its presentation clearly intended to unnerve my client.'

There was no purpose in leaving the obscene and gory photograph turned upwards any longer. The point had been made. Kay carefully turned the photograph face down as if this was not her intention at all but she knew that the image would remain in his mind.

'My apologies if your client is unnerved. Certain it will be the case that these photographs, and many others, detailed post-mortem photographs, for example, will be shown to the jury, but your comments are noted, Mr Sullivan.'

But Featherstone was unnerved particularly by the thoughts of unpleasant post-mortem photographs. He began to rub his neck, avoiding her gaze. 'But let me move on. You remarked to passengers … ,' she paused again as Mark made a point of drawing Kay's attention to some written notes, again all theatre … 'in particular Mr and Mrs Hewer-Scott, that you had, what was it, oh yes, here it is "connections in ever port" that your ship visited.'

Featherstone became anxious, irritated that this seemingly casual remark should now be used against him. 'I put it to you, Mr Featherstone that you gave the steward an envelope containing US bills to the value of 200 dollars with instructions to go to a café near the port, and there to meet a rather unsavoury character by the name of Luis Cabrera?'

'No comment,' he replied.'

But why say 'no comment'? Why not make a plausible denial thought Kay, he had had enough time to concoct one. But he was unsettled, fearful of making an unguarded comment that might incriminate him.

'Amongst the US dollar bills was a note giving Luis Cabrera instruction to ensure that Fransesco,' she said pointing to the photograph of the smiling steward, *'should never be allowed to return to the ship again?'*

There was no denial, just a question. 'And why should I do that?' he asked.

'Because the steward discovered what you were up to, Mr Featherstone. I believe this to have been on the 5th April when there was a lifeboat drill and you had to leave your cabin unattended. You see, Gerald,' she said as Mark handed her a sheet of paper detailing a matrix, 'the steward wasn't rostered to be involved in the boat drill,' adding lightly, 'he was as free as a little bird to wander about, when,' her tone changed, 'curiosity unfortunately got the better of him which ensured his hideous death.'

Featherstone was silent for a tense moment. His mind wandered. His heart rate increased, and his eyes flickered with anxiety. 'Speculation. A nonsense,' he eventually replied then added smugly, 'and you can't possibly prove any of this,' he continued with a little more confidence as if he was discussing some business deal with a friend.

'I suspect that what you perceived as nonsense, Gerald, was that whilst you were working hard, you were surrounded by pampered passengers. You were motivated by greed and envy.'

Featherstone's heart rate increased again, like an over-revving combustion engine about to blow a gasket, caused partly by the knowledge that Kay had begun to unravel his inner most motives but also because she had never before referred to him a 'Gerald'. By this stage he had become obsessed with Kay. Bizarrely he needed irrationally to impress her. He began to perspire even more.

'You might not know, Superintendent, but I am well remunerated. In fact, very well remunerated,' a smile creased his face, a stupid, irrational arrogance revealed. He felt on safe ground. Another mistake. A suspect was never on safe ground when being interviewed by Detective Superintendent Kay Yin. 'With the utmost respect, I am guessing that my annual income is much greater than yours.'

'Is that so?' asked Kay as if this fact was of little importance to her but asked in a disinterested way in order to provoke a response. She leant back in her seat.

Featherstone was determined to make a point. He was on a high roll. He *needed* to impress her. He *had* to impress her. He smiled. 'My commission last year was just shy of £140,000.'

Kay was by nature a kind person, very tolerant of others, particularly those who had fallen on hard times. She possessed no vindictiveness at all, but a young smiling man had been murdered and careful questioning would determine whether a conviction would be assured. Her over-riding sense of duty dictated that she had to encourage him to take the bait and then strike. And this was the perfect time.

'That is a very handsome sum, Mr Featherstone. And whilst you dine on board in the luxury of the *Ascot* and *Goodwood* restaurants, you must be constantly reminded of your time waiting at a café's tables, the clientele waving at you impatiently, clicking their fingers, grumbling that you had not been quick enough, that the tables weren't clean enough, pandering to their unreasonable demands and, for all your fine suits, expensive cuff-links, watches and ties,' she said leaning forward, 'you today remain in essence a shop assistant on this ship who had to leave an expensive private school and wait on tables in a coffee shop ... '

'I object most strongly to this spiteful line of questioning,' interjected Sullivan.

'The only thing that is spiteful, Mr Sullivan,' replied Kay sharply, 'was the manner of Fransesco's death. *You*, Mr Featherstone,' continued Kay in a no-nonsense tone, her eyes dark and penetrating, 'it was *you* who wrote the note to Luis Cabrera, a thug. I know for certain that you did so.'

'I did no such thing, 'he replied defiantly. But there is always a problem with lying. Telling a lie causes a tingling sensation in the delicate facial and neck tissues which will generate an involuntary need to scratch it. It can cause a slight trickle of sweat to form – and Featherstone had to scratch that too. The perspiration accentuated his after shave, hitherto *Aramis*, but today it was *Obsession* by Calvin Klein. Was this use today of a different after shave a thing of chance. Surely not. Featherstone was comforted by its use. It gave him confidence. It helped the release of *dopamine* and other brain chemicals and 'feel good' hormones. But maybe this was not such a good idea after all. When interviewed, *a person of interest* needs to be sharp and alert, not relaxed and unprepared, not simply confident and feeling good.

'Here's the thing, Mr Sullivan. On the 10th April your client visited the Accounts Department on board the *Tranquillity* where he obtained $200 in crisp bills,' Kay leaned over again removing another photograph from her briefcase. 'I am now showing Mr Featherstone Exhibit KY 36 depicting a single US ten dollar bill which the Accounts Department will tell the court was issued to Mr Featherstone, the serial number of which was recorded in compliance with the ship's money laundering protocols and produced by Cabrera when interviewed by Commissary Andrés Nájera of the International Directorate of the Mexican police.' Kay turned to Featherstone. 'It's called "insurance", Gerald.'

Featherstone looked at Kay as if he did not understand. 'Let me explain, Gerald. A crook will often retain something that he can use as a bargaining chip if he was ever to be arrested by the police or betrayed by an accomplice. Maybe you would like to explain how this thug, Cabrera, was able to be in possession of this bank note?'

'I did withdraw some cash as it happens,' blurted Featherstone, 'which I now recall I gave to the steward as a "thank you" for running some errands for me.'

'Ah, I see. Well, that's excellent. That seems to satisfactorily explain everything,' suggested Kay as if the explanation was quite reasonable. She did not question the amount nor the 'errands' but instead leaned over again and removed another photograph from her briefcase.

Then her tone changed to one that was much sharper.

'Or does it, Gerald?' Kay did not turn the photograph over but deliberately waited for a response. She looked at Featherstone with her beautiful eyes that seemed to confuse him as she waited for a reply that she knew would not come. As tense seconds ticked by he became even more anxious as he wondered what the photograph would reveal. He sat his side of the table, now full of puzzled hostility, his arms crossed and fists clenched. Moments passed.

'I am now showing Mr Featherstone Exhibit KY 38, a photograph of a hand written note that was concealed amongst the dollar bills.' Kay turned the photograph towards Featherstone. 'Let me read the note to you, Gerald, although its contents will be very well known to you:

"Make sure he doesn't get back to the ship'"

Featherstone looked as if he had suffered a cardiac arrest. 'That's not my writing,' he denied spontaneously as he looked at the grainy photograph depicting the grubby note, hoping that the lack of clarity would confuse any forensic examination.

'You are denying that you wrote this note, Gerald?' she challenged gently.

'Yes, I certainly am,' he said with a contrived but disjoined and confused confidence, adding, 'you can hardly read the writing,' he said as his mind clearly recalled the act of

[214]

writing the note whilst he now sought to diminish its value. It was an imprudent addition, an ill-considered observation of no substance, a weak attempt to understand how much of the writing could be attributed to him.

'But handwriting experts disagree, Gerald. It *is* your writing,' Kay said calmly whilst Featherstone's heart rate increased every time she called him 'Gerald' and he detected, as if in perfect unison, the scent of *Five Forty*. In unison? That would be extremely doubtful. True, he may have inhaled deeply at the mention of his name but more likely another bizarre figment of his imagination.

'I told you,' he said forcefully in the misguided hope that his robust reply would add authority to his denial, 'I did not write that note.'

Kay leaned over to her left, the emerald provocatively following as she removed Exhibit KY 23 from her briefcase. 'You will be familiar with this exhibit, Gerald.' Featherstone stared at the exhibit, transfixed, his facial expression giving all the appearance that the cardiac arrest phase had passed and rigor mortis had now already set in.

'I am now showing Mr Featherstone Exhibit KY 23, a *Certificate of Authenticity* which you gave to me, Gerald, when we purchased this emerald necklace early in the cruise from your concession on board the *Tranquillity*.' As she spoke her delicate fingers touched the necklace. Featherstone's heart rate jumped more than a few beats.

It was a rather splendid looking certificate, typed, edged in navy blue and gold, embossed with crests of *The National Association of Jewellers*, and the *British Jewellery, Gemmological and Valuers Association* together with the ship's crest.

'It is an impressive looking document, Gerald. What is even more impressive is your neat copper-plate writing detailing the necklace and signed ... oh, yes, here we are, Gerald, by *you*.'

For a moment Featherstone found himself incapable of speaking, words clogging his throat. He looked at Kay as if by producing the certificate she had somehow betrayed his fixated affection for her, a delusion of course but very real to him. He lowered his head and began to rub his eye, the brain's attempt to block out the thoughts of his behaviour. 'Our handwriting experts will testify that this note to that thug, Luis Cabrera, was written by you, although you deny this.'

Featherstone closed his eyes and threw back his head as if in surrender. His throat by now was already dry, his voice choked.

'I didn't know that they were going to kill him.'

But Kay hadn't finished with him, she needed to land him, this man who had orchestrated the brutal murder of an innocent. She spoke more gently encouraging a response.

'But how did you think that they would prevent Fransesco from returning to the ship, Gerald?'

'Just tie him up, I suppose, something like that,' he said weakly.

'And then let him go?' she offered.

'Yes.'

'But you knew that would *never* happen, Gerald,' said Kay, her tone changing as she continued relentlessly, knowing that the next few minutes would provoke the damming comments that would secure a conviction.

'*You* knew that Fransesco would always pose a danger to you. *You* knew that he could blackmail you at any time of his choosing. *You* knew that he could always ensure that you could be reduced to being a coffee shop waiter all over again, not much better than Fransesco himself.'

By now Kay knew Featherstone's history, she had the measure of him, his character and motivation and where she had to take this interview. She pushed the photograph of a smiling Fransesco towards Featherstone. Featherstone looked down at the photograph. He saw the face of a contented man, a person whom he resented, a person whom he considered had no ambition unlike himself, a person who he could not really understand but reminded him of his past, a smiling person who appeared to be mocking him.

Kay had to continue mercilessly. She had to ensure that the barbs of the hook were in deep. 'You will spend a lot of time behind bars, Gerald, where there will be plenty of time to reflect on your life.' Featherstone looked at Kay and held her gaze. Then she spoke again disapprovingly. 'You were not wealthy, Gerald, but you had a good life with the opportunity to see the world in luxurious surroundings, but you threw it all away. What a waste, Gerald. Such a waste.'

Featherstone began to tremble. Now he felt an overriding resentment at what he perceived as betrayal. Visions of his past, the unattractive parts, that he so desperately wanted to forget, returned in overwhelming clarity. He verbally lashed out at the only person he could. 'And what are you?' he shouted angrily tears beginning to sting his eyes, 'you're just a cop, that's all.'

'That's very true,' acknowledged Kay almost quietly, 'but there is a difference, Gerald,' she continued. 'You see, I shall be on the right side of the prison bars and you will be on the wrong side.'

Featherstone knew he was finished as he continued to retreat into those harsh memories of an earlier life. He sought to mentally justify his actions and blame others for his behaviour. 'I was better than he was,' he said after a short pause, his voice trembling as he pointed at the photograph of a smiling Fransesco, 'and he ... he ruined it all for me.'

'But what did he do? He was a just steward,' said Mark almost gently on cue.

Mark's question ensured that for a moment Featherstone's jumbled thoughts drifted to what was and what could have been. Eventually he spoke.

'On board ship ... ,' he began to say but then there was silence as his thoughts drifted into the past, ' ... on board ship, I was constantly, constantly bloody well reminded of what wealth can bring,' he said enviously as he starred at the smiling photograph. 'Wealth brought respect.' He began to sob. 'I couldn't go back to having no money in my pocket,' he said then simply blurted out what was uppermost in his mind. 'I had ambitions. I had a plan that could be ruined by this bloody steward who would always be a danger to me,' he said as if offering an understandable and reasonable explanation. 'He always ... always would be a danger to me and ... and I couldn't risk that. I ... I had to have him stopped,' adding almost mournfully, 'surely you can see that, can't you?'

Those were the words that Kay needed to hear to ensure a conviction: 'I had to have him stopped'.

'What I can see,' replied Kay calmly, 'is that you arranged to have Fransesco killed. What I can see is that you gave no thought to his suffering, no thought to the impact that his death would have upon his family. The only thoughts that were in your mind were of financial security and recognition, greed and self-preservation. And it will be for those reasons that you will go to prison for a long time.'

Kay pressed a buzzer on the wall. Sergeant Monk entered. 'This interview is now concluded, please take this prisoner back to his cell if you would, Sergeant.'

Featherstone contrived to delay moving towards the door so as to look for the gun on the sergeant's belt, then smirked as he acknowledged the cautious professionalism of the station staff when he saw that the sergeant was unarmed.

Would he have used the sergeant's gun on himself? Maybe, maybe not.

***

Gerald Featherstone and Andrew Craddock had never really liked each other but they did have something in common. They couldn't sleep.

Featherstone was taken to Police Cell Number 4 and placed on suicide watch. He spent most of his waking hours, which were all his hours, fantasizing with thoughts of Kay Yin and trying to calculate what the length of his prison sentence was likely to be. He even had hopes of Kay visiting him!

Craddock was placed in Police Cell Number 12, also on suicide watch. He spent his waking hours with thoughts of the fate that awaited him, not the length of imprisonment but the retribution that would be awaiting him from the drug barons.

Chapter Twenty-Six

Wednesday, 8th May 2019
Southampton, Hampshire, England

THE *TRANQUILLITY* HAD DOCKED the previous morning at 08:24 and Mark and Kay had gone on board to finalise some outstanding matters and to liaise with the local police.

Today, they met with Alivia Lace in the Southampton Harbour Hotel for lunch and were now enjoying their coffees in the Roof Top Bar with eye catching views across the Solent. Their conversation, understandably, had centred upon Craddock, Pitman and Featherstone. Alivia could understand what motivated Craddock and Pitman – greed, but she was wrestling to fully understand Featherstone's extreme behaviour and motivation.

'Most of us encounter difficulties in life,' said Mark. For a moment he fell silent, deep in reflective thought. 'I can't think of anyone,' he continued, 'who has not, whether these difficulties are health, family, finance or career related. Certainly, Kay and I have. We have all encountered what is often perceived as unfairness although very often it was simply that things just didn't work out. Most of us just roll with the punches, accept these setbacks for what they are and just get on with it. Others absorb these setbacks and convert them into something positive and meaningful and move on. Some, however, allow these matters to fester and ferment and, what shall I say, yes, corrupt judgement and behaviour.'

'And you think that is what was behind Featherstone's behaviour?'

Mark looked across towards Kay. 'Featherstone,' said Kay, 'had a comfortable start in life but then encountered difficulties, certainly not inconsequential. His mother died, their successful family business collapsed, and he had to leave his private school and became a waiter. He was feted as a bit of a local hero and became the assistant manager in a jewellery shop, but, without a positive support network, he had already begun to display signs of envy and resentment.'

'I'm guessing,' suggested Mark, 'but I think that securing the concession on board the *Tranquillity*, far from seeing it as a positive progression, it served to remind him of what he had lost. As far as we know, there was no one to offer him advice or restrain his bitterness and he began to take risks, aided and abetted by the Bristol jeweller, Bessell.'

'He was charming and capable,' suggested Kay, 'but, behind this facade lurked a pernicious dishonesty and arrogance. And he became obsessive.'

'When obsessions take primacy' said Mark, 'they usually distort judgment. He became reckless and didn't think through a sensible plan to deal with what he considered was the threat posed by the steward.'

'Like Doctor Crippen,' said Kay, 'his obsession with his lover, Ethel Le Neve, ensured that his plan to elope to the United States failed. The plan had a much better chance of success if they had travelled Third Class where he and his lover would probably have gone unnoticed amongst the cramped multitude of Third Class passengers, but his obsession with Ethel and a determination to care for her as he considered a lady should be cared, meant that he decided that they should travel First Class and, as a result, were more readily identified'.

'And George Stoner was obsessed and reckless?'

'He was certainly reckless,' Mark said. 'There was no realistic hope of him getting away with the murder of Francis Rattenbury. His arrest was inevitable.'

'Is that the key?'

'What do you mean?' asked Mark.

'Being realistic?'

'We think so. Being realistic should ensure that you don't become disappointed or maybe bitter. Some might say that we should be more ambitious,' he said looking across to Kay, they smiled and nodded to each other, 'but ambitious for what? And what do we realistic want to achieve?'

Mark poured more coffee. 'I recall visiting a retired Assistant Chief Fire Officer who had recently lost his wife. They had no children. We were seated in his rather pleasant Clifton apartment and he pointed to the mantlepiece on which was displayed his helmet badge beautifully mounted on a wooden shield alongside his Queen's Fire Service Medal for Distinguished Service and said: "Mark, it wasn't worth it." I supposed he was thinking about his life and what he had achieved. He was a lovely and capable man, but it was sad to hear.'

'But surely there's nothing wrong with being ambitious?' questioned Alivia.

'Certainly not, we need ambitious people, of course we do, but there needs to be a balance,' replied Mark.

'Balance?'

'Yes. Prince Philip wrote a book, in fact I think he wrote more than thirty, but one was entitled 'A Question of Balance'. It's a very sensible read.'

'Before we boarded *Tranquillity*,' Kay continued taking up the theme, 'we met a float plane pilot. He was realistic about what he could or could not achieve bearing in mind where he lived, his own domestic circumstances and his own desires. I think he was a realist. He recognised the limitations. His life appeared to be well balanced. Importantly, he looked around his world and acknowledged how lucky he was. He was grateful for that and content.

*****

Epilogue

Two years later.

GERALD FEATHERSTONE was convicted of Conspiracy and Complicity in the murder of Fransesco Maresca and Handling Stolen Goods. He was sentences to 17 years' and 5 years' imprisonment, the sentences to run consecutively at HMP Parkhurst, Isle of Wight.

EDWARD BESSELL, the Bristol jeweller, was arrested in respect of Conspiracy in connection with the theft of Admiral Nelson's *chelengk* and continues to assist the National Crime Agency and Scotland Yard in respect of his long-standing trafficking of unique and valuable antiques.

LUIS CABERERA was found dead in his prison cell. He had been strangled. This was a clear warning to others that disloyalty to the local drug cartel and 'private' business ventures never mix well and will never be tolerated.

ROBERT O'CONNOR aka DAVID KENNEDY was found shot dead in his red Ford Mustang behind a fish and chip shop in Portsmouth as a warning to others that failure is never an option.

THE HECKHAUSENs aka SUKHOVETSKYs were convicted at The Old Bailey, each being sentence to 42 years imprisonment and are currently serving their sentence at HMP Belmash, London under the provisions of Part 4 of the Anti-terrorism, Crime and Security Act, 2001. They continue to assist the UK National Crime Agency and MI5, the US Central Intelligence Agency and the US Drug Enforcement Agency in the penetration, arrest and conviction of the network of drug organisations within the UK, Europe and USA. Both are known to be a target of Russia's Federal Security Service for a 'wet job' - that is assassination.

ANDREW CRADDOCK was convicted of Conspiracy to Import Class A Drugs with a street value of £17,000,000 and was sentenced to six years' imprisonment, a sentence he is now serving at HMP Belmash where he is detained in the Vulnerable Prisoner Unit, known as *The Beast Wing*, for his own safety.

CHIEF SUPERINTENDENT MARK FARADAY MBE had been recommended by his Chief Constable for advancement to OBE. This had been blocked by the Home Office on the spurious grounds that Mark had failed to follow the Full Scale Decontamination Protocol and thus potentially endangering lives, and by the Foreign and Commonwealth Office who viewed his conduct as 'cavalier' with potentially adverse diplomatic consequences with their relationships with Antigua and Bermuda. These were hardly compelling reasons. The Chief Constable was still of the view that Mark's conduct had been timely and prudent, measured and ensured no panic, also ensuring the anonymity of the Russian agents, but Mark and Kay's bold success had the embarrassingly potential to overshadow the less newsworthy successes of the NCA and UK Border Force. Nevertheless, Mark continues to command the Bristol City Division and received a *Certificate of High Commendation* from Mr Justice Millard sitting in camera at The Old Bailey, London.

DETECTIVE SUPERINTENDENT KAY YIN was recommended by her Chief Constable for the award of the Queen's Police Medal for Distinguished Service. As with Mark, this award was blocked. Kay continues as the Head of Special Branch and also received a *Certificate of High Commendation* from Mr Justice Millard.

CAPTAIN ROBERT DUNBAR was appointed a MBE for his 'long standing contribution to safety at sea', an award that served, intentionally or otherwise, to preserve the reputation and commercial viability of the cruise company. He continues as Master of the *Tranquillity*.

ROBERT PITMAN gave Queen's Evidence in respect of the trial of Andrew Craddock. He was dismissed as the Assistant Chief of Security. His present whereabouts need not to be known. He remains under the protection of the UK's Protected Persons Service, part of the NCA.

ALIVIA LACE was promoted to the Chief of Security.

PROFESSOR SYBIL BODKIN continues to act as a highly respected advisor to the Devon and Cornwall Constabulary.

DESTINY WHEELER now works in a night club in Newcastle as an exotic dancer, performing under the name of 'Miss Destiny Desires'.

MR and MRS HEWER-SCOTT continue to run their successful business and regularly meet with Mark Faraday and Kay Yin.

Author's notes

Vice-Admiral Sir Horatio Nelson, Knight of the Bath, Baron of Burnham Thorpe, Viscount Nelson of the Nile and Duke of Bronte – *fact*.

HMS Victory – *fact*.

Captain Sir Thomas Hardy (later Baronet and Vice-Admiral), Captain of HMS *Victory* – *fact*.

Lady Nelson, Francis nee Nisbet, Nelson's wife – *fact*.

Lady Emma Hamilton – *fact*.

Empress Hotel – *fact*.

Francis Rattenbury – *fact*.

Alma Pekenham – *fact*.

George Stoner – *fact*.

Lieutenant-Commander Ewen Montague QC – *fact*.

Cruise liner *Tranquillity* – *fiction*.

Beachy Head statistics – *fact*.

Captain Robert Dunbar, Master of the *Tranquillity* – *fiction*.

'Williamson Turn' – *fact*.

Edmundo Gardel – *fiction*.

Nestor Virta – *fiction*.

Acapulco – *fact*.

Emeralds – *fact*.

'Five Forty' by Kurkdijan – *fact*.

Professor Sybil Bodkin – *fiction*.

St Ermine Court – *fiction*.

Burton Grange – *fiction*.

Salome Ruiz – *fiction*.

Martin Tempest – *fiction*.

'Mamas', San Francisco – *fact*.

'Flaming Coffee' – *fact*.

Pulque – *fact*.

Panama Canal – *fact*.

Colonel David Hemmings, Royal Engineers (Rtd) – *fiction*.

US General George Goethals – *fact*.

'Grey Men' – individuals who don't stand out, individuals working undercover with the security and intelligence services – *fact*.

Colombia – *fact*.

Policia Federal Minsterial, Mexico – *fact*.

Stoba Dicabrito (a stewed lamb dish) – *fact*.

Rijsttafel Keshi (a Indonesian stuffed cheese dish) – *fact*.

Pastechi (a type of pasty of beef, peppers and eggs) – *fact*.

Ayacas (a Venezuelan chicken dish) – *fact*.

Erwtensoep (a dutch soup) – *fact*.

GoldenEye – *fact*.

Antony Beckingsale – *fiction*.

Antique Roadshow Exhibits – *fact*.

French Royal Regalia – *fact*.

Crown Jewels of Ireland – *fact*.

Faberge Eggs – *fact*.

Maharaja of Patiala – *fact*.

Viscount Montgomery's Field-Marshal's Baton – *fact*.

Federal Security Service – the principal Russian security agency and successor to the KGB - *fact*.

Special Branch – the unit responsible, within local UK police forces, for gathering intelligence and mounting operations in respect of the protection of the State - *fact*.

MI5 – (the Security Service) the UK's counter intelligence and security agency – *fact*.

National Crime Agency – the UK's national law enforcement agency with a specific remit in respect of drug smuggling and organised crime - *fact*.

Captain Henry Kendal, Master of the SS *Montrose* – *fact*.

Captain (later Sir) Arthur Rostron, Master of the SS *Carpathia* – *fact*.

Captain Stanley Lord, Master of the SS *California* – fact.

Chief Inspector Walter Dew of Scotland Yard – *fact*.

Doctor Hawley Crippen – *fact*.

Ethel Le Neve – *fact*.

Section 12 (1)(a) the Aviation and Maritime Security Act 1990 – *fact*.

The Offences Against the Persons Act 1861/Criminal Law Act 1977 – *fact*.

The National Association of Jewellers – *fact*.

British Jewellery, Gemmological and Valuers Association – *fact*.

The Institute of Professional Goldsmiths – *fact*.

HMP Belmarsh, London – *fact*.

Assistant Chief Fire Officer – based on conversation with author in 1993 – *fact*.

Mr Justice Millard – *fiction*.

HRH Prince Philip, Duke of Edinburgh – *fact*.

The Superintendent Mark Faraday Collection

Available as eBook or paperback direct from
www.amazon.com.

International intrigue and brutal murder.
DIRTY BUSINESS
(set in 2008)

When one of Temporary Superintendent Mark Faraday's best young officers is murdered an intricately woven plot is uncovered involving secret bank accounts and a dissident Irish terrorist group.

From County Wicklow to the rarefied atmosphere of an exclusive London club to Salisbury Plain and the dank alleys of Bristol, and against a backdrop of brutal murder and international intrigue, a deadly clock is ticking as Mark and Helen Cave of MI5 race against time to prevent the nuclear devastation that threatens the West Country.

Heartless murder and ruthless self-interest.
DIE Back
(set in 2009)

As Superintendent Mark Faraday investigates the disappearance of a lorry driver, a top-secret US and UK intelligence operation designed to destroy the poppy fields of Afghanistan is unwittingly undermined.

But when Faraday is drawn deeper into the murky world of intelligence, he encounters cynical self-interest and murder.

From the splendour of the House of Lords to the beauty of Venetian palazzos, Mark relentlessly pursues his enquiries, haunted by the murder of one colleague and mesmerised by the beauty of another.

Treachery casts a long and deadly shadow.

Darker than DEATH

(set in 2010)

The death of a respected Bristol artist is dismissed as a bungled burglary by an unknown opportunist. But Mark Faraday is not so easily convinced.

With Detective Chief Inspector Kay Yin, Mark Faraday uncovers a web of betrayal and dishonesty that stretches back to a Belgian abattoir during November 1914 and to the very heart of present-day British government, oblivious to the betrayal and dishonesty that stalks him in his own headquarters, where loyalty by many is fleeting and deceit by some corrupting.

Espionage, treason and callous murder.

In the DARKEST of Shadow

(set in 2013)

At the scene of a fatal car accident, DCI Kay Yin finds one body with two identities. At the mortuary Kay, together with Superintendent Mark Faraday, now Head of Special Brach, discover more anomalies.

Mark and Kay's dogged enquiries take them to the Pentagon, from Rome to Gibraltar, from the savage shores of the Costa da Morte to England's south coast, where answers will be concealed in the darkest of shadows by MI5 and GCHQ, the US National Security Agency and the US Office of Naval Intelligence.

In these dark shadows Mark and Kay will encounter a callous assassin, treason and double dealing, where deception and duplicity are common place and truth an inconvenience and an allusion.

Arrogance and jealousy, treachery and murder.

DEADLY Inheritance

(set in 2015)

At the scene of a brutal stabbing, Detective Superintendent Kay Yin questions whether the deceased was the intended victim. Together with Chief Superintendent Faraday their investigation focuses upon a quartet of suspects: a successful English property entrepreneur, his Italian wife, a wine merchant from Madeira and an unsavoury Gibraltarian estate agent.

Their investigation will take them from a circus car park in Bristol to the Foreign and Commonwealth Office in London, from Gibraltar to the waters of Cabo Girao in Madeira, the extraordinary Russel-Cotes Museum in Bournemouth and the wind-swept Brecon Beacons where, at every turn they confront arrogance and egotism, envy and jealousy, treachery and hatred.

Betrayal, disloyalty and brutal murder.

In the DEAD of Night

(set in 2018)

A chance remark made by a drunk driver results in Chief Superintendent Mark Faraday and Detective Superintendent Kay Yin leading an investigation into a brutal 'cold case' murder.

Hampered by the manipulations of corruption and against a background of the heinous excesses of the German *SS* and the mafia, the secret world of the SOE Finishing School at Beaulieu and the glittering present-day Christmas festivities of the Georgian city of Bath, the dedicated officers face-down physical danger head-on, determined to unravel and penetrate the psychopathic and criminal minds of their prime suspects.

With vicious hoodlums lurking in the dark streets of rush-hour Bristol and the recesses of cafés in Malta, will their apparent casual but surgical questioning of suspects bring the perpetrators to justice?

Printed in Great Britain
by Amazon

17874947R00142